OVER the FENCE

OVER the FENCE

BY RICK STERRY

HOUGHTON MIFFLIN COMPANY BOSTON
1968

"If I were tickled by the rub of love" appeared in Dylan Thomas's *Collected Poems*. Copyright 1939 by New Directions Publishing Corporation. Reprinted by permission of New Directions Publishing Corporation.

First Printing c

Library of Congress Catalog Card Number: 68-18779
Printed in the United States of America

This is for all the past and present
full and part time members of
THE STERRY BLUEGRASS BAND

For the Mad Poet and
For the Healer

But in particular this is
For Cassie

CONTENTS

GRADU-
ATION
DAY

THE CARTOONIST AS LOVER

After several beers Daniel Blake couldn't shake the sensation that his ears were frozen or numb or missing, and he would reassure himself of their existence by pinching and twisting them or by lifting a shoulder and tipping his head and rubbing vigorously. But tonight, although both of Daniel's ears had been glowing for some time, his perversely sober mind would not stop remembering all the things that he had hoped to forget. So far he had been successful in keeping these unwanted memories out of his mind by inventing color cartoons and showing them to himself. He had long since stopped listening to the conversation of his two companions.

Right now there was no conversation. The topic which Daniel's friends had worried throughout the evening was for the moment shelved. During this silence Chevy Callister, who had been getting the worst of it, glared at the tabletop as if trying to raise two curls of smoke from its surface.

Tom Able had ordered a ham sandwich on rye bread. He had taken his first bite, and as he chewed he turned the sandwich half in his two hands, holding it like an ear of corn, examining its every angle as if selecting his next bite according to some rigid specifications.

Chevy made a short guttural sound that might have indicated either fury or despair. One of his hands came up with a quick movement and raked through his already well-tousled hair, then disappeared into a pocket, returning after a moment with a roll of tablets advertised for the soothing of unquiet stomachs. His thumb dislodged two which were tossed like peanuts into his mouth. The thumb was then brought before his eyes for an inspection of the nail — a nail chewed so short and in a thumb so squat that between them they looked like a visor-slit in a medieval helmet. Chevy squinted now at the thumb as if fighting a terrific battle within himself. To chew or not to chew.

Then abruptly he ceased to bore with his eyes at his thumb and began to bore at Tom Able. "Freedom . . ." he said passionately, coming a little way out of his chair, his arms extended wing-like to show the scope and proportion of his words. ". . . everybody has a right to act in any way . . ."

"Be a realist," Tom Able advised, chewing. "Everybody who is capable of pronouncing the word isn't necessarily capable of . . ."

"Freedom to fail, then!" Chevy said, his arms flapping. "Everybody has the right to be free to . . ."

". . . and freedom also, I suppose, to call up the Dean

and tell him to fuck himself?" This was produced calmly and without special emphasis. Tom narrowed his eyes at the last of the sandwich half; one well-placed bite separated food from art.

"She what?" Chevy sank back into his chair. "She called the *Dean of Students?* She told him . . ." Chevy began to smile.

". . . told him to fuck himself? The Dean?" Daniel had come alive. "How do you know?" he asked.

Abe looked critically at what remained of the sandwich half, holding it now in one hand, pulling his mouth unhappily to one side — a man who knows that as a sculptor in ham and rye he is doing poorly. Then his mouth straightened and his eyebrows raised philosophically. He popped it in and began chewing, looking finally at Chevy and Daniel.

"How do I know? I just know. Somebody's got to collect the facts to keep Chevy from floating off with his head up his ass." He dusted his hands together, his eyes now on the second sandwich half; matter waiting for form. He picked it up and began slowly turning it before his creator's eyes.

Chevy was smiling hugely. He had brought with him an invisible audience which was situated, apparently, slightly above him and to the right. He looked toward them. "Folks," he said, "now there's a girl who could win my heart. Can you picture it?" he asked them. "Can you picture his face? Beautiful. It's beautiful."

Daniel glowered for a moment at Chevy, annoyed to see anyone find pleasure in a world which had become so sour for him. He searched in himself for strong, bitter, devastating words with which to blast that pleasure from Chevy's grasp, but he was empty even of sarcasm and scorn.

"As usual," Abe said to Daniel, "Chevy misses the point."

Daniel said nothing.

"This missed point being that in view of this phone call, the girl hardly seems worth defending. In any case, even the most liberal court of student appeals will never seriously reconsider her expulsion now."

Daniel thought sluggishly for something to say that would strikingly jar and contradict this, but again he could find nothing. He turned away, satisfying himself with a dedicated hatred of Abe who was responsible for his being here, who had insisted that in response to the fact that the following day all three of them would graduate from college, traditional drinking should take place. It had been Abe who had brought them finally here, to the Red Carpet Supper Club and Bar.

Daniel turned in his chair, putting his gaze as far as possible from this object of his disgust and began again to look around for cartoon material, an expression on his face of someone who had held his patience far past his normal limits.

Within the Red Carpet there were two posts situated between the doughnut-shaped bar at one end of the room and the slightly raised entertainment platform at the other. Years ago, both posts had been courageously decorated to look like dwarfed elm trees complete with rather skillfully done plastic leaves, but now most of the lower foliage was gone, picked idly away by guests, and the few sparse, dust-covered leaves gave the trees an aura of fall. Daniel began to allow his imagination to play with the idea of these trees growing out of the red carpet and into the windless, winterless, smoke-filled air. He began to picture himself as an animated cartoon character, in color, dressed as a woodsman. He entered the room soberly with an ax and began to chop at one of the trees. He chopped right through the wooden center and hollered "Timber!" while people scrambled and shouted. In the cartoon Daniel showed great amazement that the tree didn't fall. He scratched his head and began to chop the other tree. He hollered "Timber!" again and the whole roof fell in. When the dust had cleared, he was standing in the middle with a contented smile on his face. "The End" flashed across his mind and he reached for his beer.

As his mind relaxed its grip on the woodsman sequence, another insistent memory attempted to force its way into the focus of his mind, but Daniel was prepared for it. He closed his eyes and drank long from his beer glass, concentrating on the feel of it in his throat, and when he set the empty glass down and filled it again from the bottle, his eyes searched quickly for something which would serve to occupy his mind. One of his hands lifted to tug first at one ear and then at the other. His tongue came out sluggishly and managed to wet both lips. He concentrated on the two men on the entertainer's platform. One man was playing an organ and smiling so that it was possible to see most of both sets of teeth, and his head bobbed on his neck like a dime-store duck. Another man was playing bass with his eyes closed, moving his pelvis toward his instrument with each beat.

After a time Daniel was surprised to discover that he was moving his feet under his chair — not in a dance movement, but in the motion of a runner, placing weight first on one and then on the other foot. He realized that he was also swaying his upper body slightly in rhythm to the pace, and he stopped this but allowed his feet to continue. In his mind the picture began to form of the galley of a slave ship. In it, at the front of countless rowing slaves, a man pounded out pace with two wooden mallets on a massive iron drum. Under the table Daniel's feet moved to this pounding, and his mind saw — in color — only the drumming. It was one of the cartoons he had used when he was a runner to preserve rhythm.

And why had Daniel become a runner?

He didn't become a runner; he had always been one. When he was a toddler his mother had been compelled to buy a leash to hold him in tow, and when he grew too old and too strong for this, he would simply run in circles around her or leave her behind. Both tricycle and bicycle had rusted unused in the garage while Daniel ran to and from school, to the swimming pool in the summer and to the skating rink in the winter. If he had shown any other peculiarities Daniel's mother might have taken him to a psychiatrist. Finally, however, as a freshman in high school, Daniel was able to satisfy his mother by channeling his personal avocation into a Supervised, Authorized and Acceptable Group Activity. He went out for the track team.

That spring when Daniel was a freshman at West Jefferson High at Easton, there had been a boring period of indoor workouts and gymnasium running, and then Coach had finally taken the team to the big oval. He lined up the distance runners and paced before them hands on hips, silver whistle dangling on his gray sweat shirt, red face glowering. "Now let's see who the hell can run around here," he snarled. "Let's weed out the candy-asses. I wanna separate the puny-peckers from the swingin' dicks right away."

He was the most popular coach in the history of the school.

During that first outdoor workout Daniel easily won both the mile and the half mile without really exerting himself. For a freshman this was entirely unprecedented, but Daniel was not at all surprised. He had thought about it and he suspected that he was the best boy runner in the world. Later in the locker room Coach had punched him on the arm and had spoken favorably of Daniel's testicles — an unheard-of favor. Daniel did not allow himself to be especially moved. He was prepared to be unchanged by success.

But at practice a week later success faded. Daniel watched in amazement as three upperclassmen pounded past him in the final leg of the mile, and a half dozen runners finished the half before he did.

Daniel made the team that year, as he did during his sophomore, junior and senior years, and as he had during three years at Easton College, but he had never won a race. Every year he worked a little harder, trained a little more religiously, conditioned more rigorously than the year before, and each year he improved only enough to enable him to make and remain on the team. He resigned himself to the fact that he would never win. Daniel still liked to run, and he enjoyed the discipline of the training. Once he had overheard the coach at Easton say that had any other athlete he had ever coached developed his natural abilities to the peak of their potential as Daniel had, that athlete would have been a champion.

It was all the recognition Daniel wanted or needed.

But now, sitting under the plastic tree, his feet slowly ceased to run and the vision of the galley ship faded. The memory he had tried to avoid with beer and cartoons began another replay in his mind.

He had gone to pick up Ellen from her office after she finished work. He had found a good parking place not fifty paces from where she would exit, and had settled himself with a magazine to wait. Finally she had opened the door and without saying a word threw a booklet toward him. It fell on the open pages of the magazine he'd been reading. On its cover letters of the alphabet, having sprouted feet and hands and smiling mouths, danced and spelled YOUR FIRST BABY.

It was like lights going out for Daniel. He hadn't even thought it possible. He couldn't take his eyes from the letters. He was afraid to look up at Ellen's face.

"You sure?" he said finally, and he looked up at her.

"You ever been told a lie by a rabbit?" she asked, tears glinting in the corners of her eyes. Her laugh turned into a terrible whimper.

He turned his face away from her, his eyes widening

blankly. Well, here it was. Here it finally was. Daniel had an impulse to take a deep breath.

"Damn, damn, damn, damn," said Ellen on the other side of the car. Her hands rose to cover her eyes and her voice skidded into the whimper again. Daniel sat, his hands clutching the magazine, staring vacantly out the front window. On the street traffic roared and within his head great blocks shifted slowly, making room for this new fact. One of the most important things in his life was happening to him. He was going to marry this girl who sat with him in the front seat of this car. He had fathered a child that she carried. Her whimper had now increased to heavy sobs.

"All right," he said gently. "It'll be all right." He reached out for her hand.

"All *right!*" She turned a face full of violence toward him. "All *right?* Have you been listening? I'm *pregnant!*"

He decided not to notice. "Listen," he said, clearing his throat patiently. "You know that I'll marry you. You know that, don't you?" He began to reach for her shoulder, then changed his mind and put his arm on top of the seat. "Look, I mean the thing to do is accept the situation and work from that point. The reason you're so upset . . ."

"Daniel . . ." she said in a small voice, beginning to rock in the seat, "for God's sake . . ."

"You mean you don't want to get married to me? Ellen, we tal . . ."

"Oh, *shit!*"

"We talked about it before and . . ."

"What I don't want to be is *pregnant!*" She reached out her arms to brace herself against the dashboard as if to keep her body from some great violence. *"I don't want to be pregnant!"*

He looked at her a long time while her voice died out of the car. "You *are* pregnant," he said as quietly as he could, ". . . and so let's proceed from there." He watched her for several long seconds. "Now there are some things we *can* do and there are some things we *must* do."

"Daniel . . ."

"First, we must avoid being emotional."

"Daniel . . . Daniel please, not now." Her voice became small and she brought her hands from the dash to cover her eyes again.

"Not now what?" Daniel said patiently.

"Don't talk about it *that* way."

"What way?"

"Like it was a *prob*lem to be solved . . ."

"Well, it *is* a prob . . ."

"But that's not all. That's not all it is."

"Ellen, I'm not sure . . ."

"How do I know . . ." she took a deep breath and pressed her eyes and started over. "How am I supposed to know if you love me? How do you know that I love you? Do you even care about that?" Her voice had begun to skid again.

"You want me to be dramatic? Is that it? I could thrash all over the front seat and work myself into a tearful ecstasy and still hate your guts."

"And you could be kind and considerate and thoughtful

and hate my guts too, sweetheart." He had not noticed when it had happened, but she was now cold and tearless.

They were pressed against the opposite ends of the car. He absently tested the smoothness of the steering wheel with his index finger and thumb.

"Don't you think," he said finally in a weary voice, "that I have any intellectual integrity? By this time you should be able to know if you can trust the things I say."

"I trust the things you say," she said quickly. "When you say you'll marry me I believe you. I'd also believe you if you looked me in the eye and said you loved me and wanted the baby. You haven't done that yet."

He was quiet for a long time, staring out the window. Finally he let a long hiss of air out between his teeth. "If you don't know I love you," he said, ". . . then where the hell have you been for the last few months?"

She let her head slide against the glass, and in full view of the people passing on the street, she began to cry openly. "It's different now," she said. "I thought I knew, but it's different now."

"No, it isn't different. Why should it be different? Don't crowd your head with that True Romances crap." He was attempting to keep his voice as mild as possible. He reached up nervously and adjusted the rear-view mirror. "Look," he said. "If you're waiting for me to make the first move, then I'll make it." Daniel didn't plan it, but his voice deepened at this point. "I would prefer that we got married," he said.

"You'd prefer it?" she asked incredulously. "You'd *prefer* it?"

"You know what I mean, Ellen, don't cloud the issue, okay?" His chest heaved with his efforts at self-control. He clenched and unclenched his fingers on the steering wheel.

"Yes," she said. "I think I do know what you mean. I think I *do*." Her voice skidded.

"Please!" he said. "Please! You're talking like somebody in a bad movie. Please stop it. This is too serious to play . . ."

"Say you love me then."

"Listen," he said, and he straightened in the seat, choosing words carefully. "I refuse to sully the gravity of the situation by pretending we're characters in a bad . . ."

"You can't," she said. "You can't say it. There's no love in you. Nothing. There's nothing in you at all." She was shaking her head sadly, pity in her voice.

He was silent a moment, his mouth moving experimentally. "Crap!" he said finally, turning back to the window. He heard the door-latch click.

"I'm going," she said. "Don't bother to call."

They both hesitated for a fraction of a second.

"Ellen," he said. "You call me when you think you're ready to talk about it like an adult."

She left the car, not slamming the door, but shutting it in a way that had more finality.

It had taken him only ten minutes to drive home, and in that time the full weight of the situation had settled on him. A half hour later he had tried to call her, and in the two days since then he had called twenty or thirty times more. He had even driven to her home twice, but she would not see him or talk to him. Four hours of drinking had not erased the guilt he felt.

He turned himself now violently in his chair as if turning from something offensive and focused determinedly on the conversation of Chevy and Abe, trying to empty his mind of everything but words.

"Because . . ." Abe was saying in a calm but tired voice, ". . . because a college is responsible first to the parents. The parents, after all, are the ones who . . ."

"It should be responsible first to the *stu*dents!" Chevy said. "The *stu*dents! The value structure of the students is the only viable . . ."

"But it's the parents who pay the bills, and, right or wrong, it's the man with the dollar who gets to make the rules. It's the Great American Way, baby. The administration has no choice. If you were in charge wouldn't you impose your value structure on them? Wouldn't you insist . . ."

"Hell no, I wouldn't."

"You wouldn't, huh?" Abe leaned back in his chair in a defeated way.

"No, I wouldn't."

"Well, I just hope to Christ we never get a chance to find out if you would or not." Abe began to look disinterestedly around the room, signaling an end to the conversation. The Red Carpet had been filling steadily in preparation for the performance of the feature entertainer, and many of these guests at surrounding tables were staring frigidly at Abe's table in response to the loudness of Chevy's half of the argument. Tom Able smiled and nodded amiably at those who met his eyes, sipping his beer.

For several moments Daniel had been rubbing a shoulder meditatively against an ear, and now he leaned suddenly forward. "Hey, listen," he said to neither one in particular. "Would you say that I'm an unemotional person? I mean, you guys 've known me for years. Would you say that I was basically kind of a reserved person or what? I mean . . ."

Chevy had been sitting in an attitude of dejection, but now he straightened. Between his eyebrows a severe line formed. "What the hell does that mean? Unemotional — what does that mean? It's what you do that makes the difference. It's the action." Chevy began to stab a finger toward Daniel. "Take this week when I needed help for this girl. Nobody wants to get involved. Everybody wants to sit around discussing the issues involved." Chevy looked pointedly at Abe, and Abe smiled.

Daniel wet his lips several times before speaking, surprised to find how much his tongue had thickened since the last time he had spoken. "But that wouldn't mean that people don't have emotions," he said. "People can tear themselves apart inside and not show it. Just because they don't make a goddamned display . . ."

"If a person feels something, he should validate that feeling with action. Listen! Do you think that the good and the right are going to triumph just because they're the good and the right? Listen! Take this poor girl! Something has to be done!"

"I mean, would you say that if a person doesn't act that

means he has no feeling?" Daniel's words had a rubbery unsteady sound, as if they were carved gracelessly from pieces of gum eraser.

"No! Hell no, Daniel! That's the point." Chevy began to jab his finger violently into the table. "It's what you do with your feelings. *Some* bastards turn them into words, like Abe, or into some other safe son-of-a-bitching thing out of fear."

"Fear," Daniel said slowly, his eyes suddenly glassy and empty like the eyes of a man before whom a vision has appeared.

"Fear!" affirmed Chevy. "Damn right!" He glared at Abe and reached an unsteady hand toward his beer glass.

Daniel began to see. He lifted up his hands involuntarily and gripped his ears, sitting rigid and tense in his chair. Yes! he said to himself, Yes! It was not that there was no emotion, it was that there was too much. Yes! It was by their very excess that his emotions demanded restraint. Just as strong men must cultivate mildness for the protection of themselves and others, so had he cultivated restraint. Yes, out of fear!

Daniel's hands remained locked and forgotten on his ears. He was realizing that he must overcome this fear, and the words and symbols that held this realization were coming with blinding speed and intensity.

Of course, he said to himself. Of course! Rejection of the emotions is wrong. Control! Control is the answer. Emotions must be regulated, not repressed.

Daniel began to see that he had been wrong to have demanded that Ellen produce only genuine and perfect emotions when he had not had the courage to produce any emotions at all, and at this thought there was a tug at the corners of his mouth and something expanded in his throat and his eyes began to mist. At least she had tried, he told himself. Though her choice had been wrong and the emotions imperfect, she had at least tried.

Daniel's mouth was oddly open and his breath became labored. He pushed a thick, sluggish tongue over his lips and brushed away the mist with the heel of his hand, admitting to himself the hardest thing of all. He had not even been able to try.

Was it too late then? he asked himself. Was the habit of repression — the fear — was it too firmly embedded? Was it too late to change? Too late to prove to the world the genuine emotions that were inside him? Too late to prove the love that he felt?

Daniel knew that he must answer that question and that he must answer it now. He knew that he must test himself. He must do now what he had not been able to do with Ellen. Only this would make him worthy of her — and of the child.

Daniel focused his eyes on his two friends. His lips formed words and he raised his hand to speak . . .

"Son-of-a-bitch!" Chevy jumped to his feet, brushing at his lap with both hands. Daniel righted the glass automatically with the hand that had upset it and he began to stand, but his right leg seemed asleep — responsive, but retarded. If Abe's hand had not caught him he would have fallen.

"Hey!" Daniel said. He settled himself slowly back into his chair with a surprised expression. "Hey, Chevy, I'm really sorry. Damn leg's asleep or something." Daniel began to pound experimentally on the thigh of the unresponsive leg.

"Folks," Chevy looked up and a little to the right. "Does that explain why his hand splattered beer all over me? Now I ask you . . ."

"Drunk," said Abe without expression. "Drunk in record time."

"Drunk?" Daniel looked suddenly frightened. "No! Look, *any*body can spill a beer. Look, it's important that you realize that I am definitely, definitely, *def*initely not . . ."

"Drunk!" Abe pronounced. "Daniel, you're drunker 'n seven hundred barrels of owl puckey."

They could not think him drunk. Not now, not when he was perhaps more aware than ever before in his life. Not now, when for the first time he knew exactly and precisely what he was doing. "Look," he said, and he showed Abe and Chevy wide bright eyes and a sincere expression. "I could drink all night yet. I probably *couldn't* get drunk." He held his arm in the air and snapped his fingers as if summoning final proof. "Waiter," he said. "Three more."

"Daniel, learn your capacity," Chevy said. "You drink another beer you're gonna barf."

Daniel leaned across the table and spoke gravely, patiently. "I am definitely, definitely, *def*initely not drunk, and it's important that you believe me." He spoke his words in little groups, tapping emphasis on the table with his fingers. "I have a very important, important thing to say." He took a deep breath . . .

A waitress appeared and slowly began to clean the spilled beer from the table. Daniel watched, the corner of his mouth curling spasmodically twice as she finally finished and stepped back.

"Did I see another round here?" she asked the plastic tree in a lead-colored voice.

"What?" said Daniel, his voice with an edge like a bread knife, his mouth jerking again.

"Another round here?" She threw her weight on one hip, still looking at the tree with a weary patience.

"Obviously!" Daniel dipped the word in steaming poison and handed it to her with red-hot tongs. She shrugged.

"Whew!" Abe said. "Mean drunk."

"I'm not drunk! Not! Not! Not! Now I've got something important to say, and I'm gonna say it. Okay, you bastards?"

"Hey, Daniel," Chevy said. "I think your tongue is going to sleep just like your leg."

Daniel nodded slowly. "Okay!" he said. "You don't wanna listen? Fine with me."

"What 've you got to say, Daniel? Really, hey?" Chevy slapped the table for attention. "C'mon, Dan. We were kidding."

"Screw you!" Daniel said, bowing slightly from the waist in his chair.

"I'm sorry, Dan. Hey, bad joke. Really. Quick! If you got something to say, you better speak up before you start to barf all over. Quick! Quick!"

Then suddenly the lights were gone out of the room except for a small cone on the entertainer's platform. Into this cone stepped a man who squinted and wrestled with the microphone, pretending that he was alone in the room. He slid the microphone up and down, searching for some unknown level. Finally he locked it into place, shaded his eyes and exhibited great surprise to find that the room was full of people.

"Well, ladies and gentlemen," he said, clasping his hands in front of him. "I guess you all know what we got here for you tonight at *thee* Red Carpet." He looked shy for a moment, tilting his head to the side, then he began to look directly at the microphone head, talking earnestly to it as if it were an attentive ear. "Well," he said, "we have a wonderful young lady here tonight. A Great Artist and a Truly Great Star of *thee* motion pictures, teevee, records and aaaagh — "

He looked seriously at his hands as clouds of blue smoke entered the silent circle of light with him. "— and of *thee* motion pictures." He smiled abruptly at the ceiling. "She is with us here tonight at thee Red Carpet after a tri*um*phant tour of *thee* West Coast, and, aaaagh, and aaaagh — a tri*um*phant stay in Las Vegas. She comes to us here tonight from — from aaaagh . . ." his eyes widened blankly and for several seconds the sound of his breathing came to the audience with hi-fi clarity. Then he remembered. ". . . direct from Las Vegas, and *thee* Red Carpet is proud to *present* . . ." He hurled his arm to the side, the gesture and the smile frozen for several seconds while something Big did not happen. He turned finally back to the audience and was avalanched by the belated drum roll. He fled.

Into his place a second later stepped the Truly Great

Star herself, wearing around her neck a guitar which was mostly covered with her name inlaid in pearl. She stood smiling for several seconds while the polite applause died down. The lights came up on the platform and it was seen that the bass man now played an electric guitar while the organ man's head bobbed behind drums. Both wore sequined jackets which matched that of the Truly Great Star. The three burst simultaneously into the same song.

Daniel saw and heard nothing. On his face played the inward-turned, distant expression which Martin Luther might have presented as he raised the hammer, or which an observer might have seen on the face of Moses as he returned from the burning bush. Daniel's hands were white-knuckled in his lap. Within him wave after wave of emotion swelled and burst. He knew that this emotion must be contained no longer, that its release would bring back Ellen, would issue in a new life. Several times he took in great breaths of air and poised his mouth for speech. Then the breath would be released and his tongue would flicker over his ash-colored lips.

Suddenly his hands leaped from his lap to grip the edge of the table and he leaned forward. "Love . . ." he whispered, then with another breath, in another louder voice, "Love is the . . ."

Chevy raised himself from the table. " 'Scuse me! Just a second, Dan. Kidneys. Excesses of my youth. Be right back." He began to leave his chair.

"*Listen!*" Daniel pounded the table a great pound. Chevy sat slowly back into his chair while Abe and many others gave Daniel their undivided attention. On the stage the Truly Great Star began to molest "Dark Moon" unconcernedly. Around Daniel's table stillness reigned while Daniel formed words with great gulps of air. "Listen," he gasped, "I'm gonna . . . it's always been hard for me to . . . yesterday Ellen . . . I'm in . . ."

"Three beers," said a lead-colored voice behind him.

"Listen . . ." Daniel half rose from his chair, his eyes never leaving his two friends as he fumbled in his pocket. "I've got to tell you this, I love . . ."

"Three beers," insisted the leaden voice.

Daniel swept his arm back wildly, attempting to sweep away the voice. "I'm *proud*," he said, "I *love* . . ."

"Listen, buddy, you ordered three beers here, and I . . ."

"ELLEN'S GOING TO HAVE MY . . ."

"Here!" said Chevy, holding money toward the girl.

"Here!" said Abe, tearing at his back pocket for his wallet.

"Going to have my . . . have my . . ." Daniel's voice became a low moan, dying slowly.

"One-fifty out of five," said the girl efficiently, taking Chevy's money and jingling in her apron for change.

"Dark Moooooon," sang the Truly Great Star,

> Way up high, up in the sky,
> Oh tell me why, oh tell me why
> I lost yer favorrrrrrrr?

Daniel was sitting back in his chair, his head low toward his knees. He was making a sound.

"What?" asked Chevy, leaning down.

"Dark Mooooon," sang the Star.

"AAAAAUUUUUUUGGgggghhgghgggh!" said Daniel between his knees.

Behind the Great Star the electric guitar man came to life, his eyes searching the audience. Great Star sang on, an expression on her face like a sheet of clean paper.

Oh tell me why, oh tell me why
I've lost his luuuuuuuuvve.

"OOOOOOOAAAAAAAAUUUGGgghhhgggrrrl," said Daniel, helplessly splattering the deep red rug.

For the rest of the song he continued his duet, until finally, his breath returning to his own control, he lifted his head from between his legs and called out to his friends.

"Abe?" he rasped. "Chevy?"

But he was alone.

II

When Daniel arrived weakly at the car outside the Red Carpet, his friends were still howling. They were beating the dash with their fists and they were thrashing back and forth, replaying the scene complete with sound effects furnished by Abe while Chevy sang. When it was possible to be heard Daniel began to curse. "You bastards," he whispered, "take me home."

"Home?" said Abe. "What's this self-destruction thing you're on? It's early, ol' buddy. You'll never get past your mother."

"Fuck my . . ." Daniel began.

"What you need is a good ol' bowl of good ol' chili," Abe said over the seat to him. "Now I just happen to know of a place where the chili has special sobering properties and where the waitress will interest ol' Chevy. How about a bowl of good ol' chili?"

In the back seat Daniel made a negative sound, but the car roared away unheeding.

When Abe stopped outside Beanie's Chili Parlor, Daniel refused to be moved. He lay chattering on the back seat, his arms hugging himself in the warm spring air, kicking fitfully at the friendly hands which reached to take him out of the car. Finally, still giggling, they shrugged and left him.

After a few minutes another prolonged violent sound issued from the back seat, and shortly after that Daniel rose slowly to a sitting position. The events of the Red Carpet began to pass slowly and with dreadful clarity through his mind. It had been a night of searing revelation.

A sickly laugh rose from him and he let his head roll to the side until it collided with the window of the car. What was he to do then? He had tried and he had failed. Better, he thought, to be dry. Better to be devoid of emotion than to feel it surge within you and be unable to let it out. Daniel began to beat slowly and solemnly against the window with his head, a small, wire-thin, tight-lipped sound coming from his mouth. Love was gone. Friends . . . self-respect — all, all gone. When had it happened? When had it all begun? How? He began to twist viciously at the lobe of one completely numb ear. When had he been tricked into selling his birthright of honest emotional response for the bland, saltless pottage of restraint? Restraint! It was his mother's word, and it seemed to Daniel that it was her voice that pronounced it now in his mind.

Daniel stopped the motion of his head. For the second time of the evening he received a revelation. It was his *mother!* It was *She* who was responsible for what he had become. It was his mother who, when he was a helpless child, had planted the seeds of restraint in his mind!

Now, here in the back seat of Abe's car he realized for the first time that for years he had simply waited for all this to change — waited for something to happen which would change everything and free him. And it was happening *Now.* It had begun *now!*

Daniel began to move in the back seat. Finally the door opened and he spilled to the ground. He rose slowly. It was clear to him now where the guilt lay. It was his own fear of his mother that had caused him for two days to fight against accepting the truth. It was fear of her that caused him to reject Ellen when she needed him the most. She! His mother! She was responsible.

Leaning against the car, Daniel brought both fists to his temples and loosed a great cry against the loins that had borne him and the pap which had given him suck.

His course of action was clear. He steadied himself and took his bearings. He realized that his body was drunk, uncontrollable, disheveled and soiled, but Daniel knew also that this body contained within it a mind clear and clean as flame. He spread his arms wide and laughed a terrible laugh. What irony. What justice that his mother, who had always been deceived by appearances, who could never see the beauty within — how fitting that she should see him like this. How fitting! How proper!

Daniel began to run, elbows high, through the city of Easton and toward home. He ran twelve blocks straight down Eighth Avenue, running broken-field through the people spilling from the Easton Theater. He turned his eyes neither to the right nor to the left. At Thirteenth Street he turned and ran for eight more blocks. He stopped for nothing; he saw nothing but cold necessity. As he ran his mother's face bobbed before him urging caution, control, reserve, and Daniel repeated "Screw you, cha cha cha. Screw you, cha cha cha," in his mind, thus preserving the running rhythm and drowning out the nagging voice in the back of his mind which called for caution or at least for planning. Daniel was not to be delayed. The force which stirs a man to run screaming, hand grenade in either hand into an enemy gun emplacement — the siren voice which urges the bull moose to charge the dump truck — these drove Daniel's legs.

Daniel did not stop. He did not break pace until with a final leap he gained the front steps of his mother's house.

When Mrs. Blake looked up and noticed that her only son stood panting and sweat-soaked in the middle of her living-room rug — when she noticed that his eyes were horribly bright and that his face was twisted in a strange expression — when she saw these things she did not so much as uncurl her still trim ankles from under her, nor did she close the book she was reading. She lowered her head slightly and peered at him over the top of her reading glasses.

Mrs. Blake had not achieved her many successes by making emotional displays at every apparent crisis. The gaze she turned on her son was one of clear-eyed self-possession and contained an honest but not inordinate curiosity. It was this same kind of clear-eyed intelligence and sweet-scented honesty that struck numbing terror into the hearts of her business associates and competitors even as it called forth the best that was in them. Men know how to handle other men who are as potentially dishonest as themselves, just as women know how to handle other women who are as vain or as greedy. But nobody knew just how to handle Daniel's mother.

Somewhere in his childhood everyone has found it necessary to create for himself a mother without flaw; a mother who is loving but stern, fair but exacting, who knows and forgives our weaknesses, but who also knows our secret strengths and sees the untapped reservoir of our goodness. It was to her we turned when our real mothers failed us, and as the years went by and our needs changed, we altered this creation, but we never abandoned it. We jealously carried it, still faceless, still formless, into our adulthood.

Daniel's mother gave this image face and form. She presented herself to the eye as that ideal made sudden flesh, and the startled mind did not doubt for an instant that it was she. Grown men, otherwise self-assured and self-possessed, lords among their own sex, would shift and squirm before her like truants caught in naughtiness. Under the conference table at which she was present, fifty-dollar shoes would cross one over the other and within them toes would curl. Women who had approached her with their hearts full of poison would, under her smile, giggle and primp and stand on their toes like schoolgirls.

In the business world this was a powerful advantage, and Mrs. Blake combined it with a shrewd mind and a bartender's memory of names and faces. She understood perfectly the elements at the root of her successes, and she chose styles, stance, walk and even eyeglasses to augment what nature had provided. Her careful nurturing of her gift had given her the most thriving real-estate business in the city; and in the next election it would very likely place her in high public office.

One does not betray the goose that lays such golden eggs. If sacrifices are called for, one makes them.

Sacrifices, of course, were called for. When she lost her husband to another woman, Mrs. Blake lost the only two people whom she had allowed to see the real human being behind the social appearance; and with them gone there was no one to suspect that she was more than an impossible actualization of an unapproachable ideal.

"What seems to be the trouble, Daniel?" she asked. Her voice was well controlled. "Is something wrong?"

"Wrong?" Daniel said hoarsely, his breath short. "You damn bet something's wrong." He threw his suit coat and tie toward a chair, missing. In the tastefully furnished, flawlessly arranged room it fell in a heap. HE HAD BEGUN! IT WAS HAPPENING! A thousand bugles began to blow in his head.

Mrs. Blake swung her ankles to the floor and set her book carefully on the coffee table in front of her. It was evident to her that nothing serious was wrong — no one hurt or killed. Her son was, she saw, very drunk.

"Well?" she said, settling herself for something unpleasant.

"You better sit the hell down, Mother dear, because I'm going to say some things you might not like to hear." He curled his lips, leaning toward her. "They might just be a little shocking."

Mrs. Blake looked meaningfully toward the couch where she sat, then back at her son, her eyebrows slightly arched. He appeared not to notice.

"And if it's a little shocking maybe that's just all right." He took a step toward her ominously, daring her to contradict. "Maybe we'll shock loose a few changes around here."

Daniel's mother noticed a long smear of gray, moist-looking particles clinging to the left pant-leg of her son's slacks. The smear ran from just below the pocket to the knee. She flinched inside herself and wondered if it would dry-clean.

Daniel had begun to pace, his face contorted with thought. "Now listen!" he said. He was pounding one fist into the palm of his other hand.

"Daniel . . ." his mother began, taking her glasses off and folding them carefully. "I don't know . . ."

"You're damn right you don't know. You don't know *shit!*"

What was happening in front of her was so far outside

any possible expectation of what might happen that Mrs. Blake began to have the feeling that she was caught somewhere between a real situation and a dream, as if she had found herself suddenly in the plot of the thriller she had been reading.

"This shouldn't be so hard for me," Daniel was saying, his eyes filling up with tears. "It shouldn't." He turned full toward her, blinking, his jaw a hard but quivering line. "You're my goddamned mother. Why can't I talk to you? Why can't I talk to anybody? Show my emotions?" He stopped to get his breathing under control. He put his arms out, Christ-like — crucified. "What is life without real emotions?" he asked. "Yesterday I found out something so important that it'll change my whole life, and I . . . I . . ." His mouth jerked for a second, then closed, and he took a step toward her, capable for a second of something violent.

"Daniel . . ." his mother began.

"Shut up!" he hissed. "Listen to *me!* To *me!* You never listen. *Listen!* You want to know what I found out yesterday? You want to know?" He was breathing through his mouth, his nasal passages closed with tears. " — and you know what I did? Nothing! *Restraint!*" He shook a fist, his teeth clenched. "I lost her," he said, ". . . because of you!"

He paused, blinking away tears. He took a deep breath and stepped back and looked his mother coldly in the eyes, standing tall, erect. "Mother," he said. "Yesterday I found out that . . ." He took several deep and labored breaths, his eyes locked with hers. "I found out, by God that" — and his voice reached a crescendo — "I'm PREGNANT!"

Mrs. Blake sat frozen for several seconds, staring at the breathless boy in front of her.

"Hah!" the boy said, striking the butts of his hands to his temples. He staggered backward with the blow, reeling. "I knew it," he said. "You're just like me. Cold! There's nothing in you." His words were high and desperate. He staggered, fists over both eyes, circling blindly like Oedipus. "My God, Mother, aren't you even interested? Aren't you moved? Aren't you going to say anything? Don't you even want to know who's going to be my wife?"

His mother had been watching him as one watches the hypnotist's spinning watch. His voice came to her from far away. She forced her eyes from him, her mouth moving tentatively as she tried to form words. She clasped her hands tightly in her lap, squeezing them together until the knuckles were white. "Certainly I do," she said. "Yes, of course." The impulses to laugh and cry swept alternately over her.

"It's a girl named Ellen! Ellen!" He had mastered his breath now, and his lips flared suddenly back over his teeth. "And I'm gonna marry her, by God, whether you like it or whether you don't."

"Of course," his mother said distantly. Her son was getting married. It came to her like the solution to a puzzle. He was getting married to a girl named Ellen. He was bringing home a wife. There would be a family. A family! He had fathered a child. The news spread through her body like brandy.

"Mother, for God's sake, don't you care?"

"Oh, yes," she said, her voice small, preoccupied, excited. "Oh, Daniel, *yes*." She wondered who this Ellen might be. She wondered what kind of a girl she might be.

"Don't you try to stand in my way," her son said. "She's every bit as good as you are!"

"Yes, yes, I'm sure she is, Daniel. Oh, *yes*." She would like this girl, she thought. She would love her — Daniel's wife. Something like Christmas bells moved through her blood.

"Her family doesn't eat from fine china every day, but they don't . . ." Daniel's sneer dissolved, and he turned suddenly away.

His mother began to tremble. Whatever this girl had not had, she would have it. She would have everything. Everything! Within her Mrs. Blake's heart swelled until she felt she must bring her hand to cover the place. "Oh, Daniel," she said. She rose and moved toward him. "Oh, Daniel, I'm so happy."

"*Balls!*" roared Daniel, turning on her like an enemy in the dark. "You don't think I know you by now? How the hell dumb you think I am? That's your way, isn't it? Pretend to go along with me. Pretend to agree, then before I know what I'm doing, I'm agreeing with what *you* want." He pointed a rigid, quivering forefinger toward her. "You insidious . . . insidious . . ." He stood there, finger shaking; then, as if exhausted with the exertion needed to produce the next word, his eyes went blank and his hand dropped. He moved suddenly toward his suit coat on the floor and snatched it up.

For the first time in many years instinct overpowered Mrs. Blake. "No!" she said. "Daniel, I'm happy. *Happy!* I *want* you to marry Ellen!" The name was already delicious on her tongue.

Daniel backed away, his face suddenly white. "Stay away from me. I know what you're doing." At his side he made a white-knuckled fist. Then abruptly he threw his head back and laughed. The fist unfolded at his side and came up to cover his eyes for a second. "You *want* me to marry Ellen? Oh, God, Mother!" He leaned against the wall by the door and howled with laughter. "What a ball-buster that is." He stopped laughing and leaned toward her, a sudden lucid intelligence on his face. "How can you want me to marry Ellen if you *don't know who she is?*"

His mother stood silent before him, her eyes large, her hands making little flipper motions at her sides. "Daniel . . ." she said finally, her voice not steady. "If you've chosen her, then I know that she must . . ."

"Mother," Daniel shouted, "I didn't *choose* her, *I knocked her the hell up!*" He pressed the heels of his palms to his forehead. "You *never, ever listen* to me!" He held his hands on his head, bent back as if recovering from a stunning blow, while he walked in small circles in front of the door.

"All right," he said finally, "if that's the way you want it, that's the way it'll be." His eyes looked for something upon which he could bring down his fist in a gesture of finality. There was nothing.

"Daniel . . ." His mother took an uncertain step toward him.

"Shut the hell up," Daniel said, a cutting, icy edge in his voice. "We don't need your approval. I got a college goddamned education, you know. I don't need you. We'll go the hell off someplace where you can't change everything." He stared at her briefly, then turned to the door. He opened it and whirled toward her again. "If you can't accept my wife," he snarled, "then how the hell can you accept me?" He turned again to go out, and his mother, emotionally battered as never before, wondered wildly what to do. Constitutionally she could not be left like this, on the open end of a *non sequitur*, and there was the unbearable thought that perhaps, after all, he would really go away. Perhaps he would take Ellen from her and never come back.

"Daniel!" she said, and he stopped. "Daniel, whatever I've done I'm sorry for." Her voice quivered dangerously. Daniel did not turn back to her, but he did not leave, either. Daniel waited. "Daniel," she said. "I'll give you any house on my roster. For you and . . . and Ellen. Any house. We'll begin looking any time you want. You and I and Ellen, we'll begin to look tomorrow. Any house at all. Please believe . . ." Her voice broke with a small sound like a piece of delicate glass. She brought her hand to her mouth, but it had started and it could not be stopped. Tears leaped to her eyes. Her energy drained from her and she took uncertain steps toward the couch.

By the door her son smiled a strange smile, and without speaking or turning, left.

BEANIE

Beanie's Chili Parlor was narrow and high, shaped like a matchbox on edge. Between the counter on one side and the row of high-backed booths on the other there was just enough room for a black, tarry path to be worn through the linoleum pattern.

Few people remembered the fact, but at one time Beanie's had been the site of the most exclusive women's fashion store in Easton, and it had been owned by a French woman who spoke in a heavy, and some said inconsistent, accent. But fifteen years ago when the new Highway 176 had been put down Eighth Street rather than down First Street as expected, the business center of town had moved and left the area around the French woman's shop as deserted as an Arizona cliff dwelling.

Today, sharing the same side of the once fashionable and impressive street with Beanie's were two bars, a small grocery, the Salvation Army store, two secondhand shops, the Jesus Saves Mission, and one other restaurant besides Beanie's.

Beanie himself, according to his own story, had settled in Easton purely by accident. He had been traveling through selling Bibles, heading west toward the back country where people still bought them in the illuminated, leather-bound family editions. Beanie had no intention at all of stopping at Easton. The decision had been made for him by three hoboes who appeared in Beanie's boxcar at the stop just before Easton. They had taken the suitcase containing his black suit of Bible-selling clothes, his order blanks, his sample Bibles, and the partial plates for the fronts of his upper and lower teeth. They had also efficiently taken the clothes from his back, and without even bothering to look in the suitcase had thrown Beanie naked and toothless from the train as it slowed to enter Easton.

The teeth had been tied neatly in a handkerchief and hidden inside the suitcase before he boarded the train. He found it necessary to travel toothless since a lot of gold showed when he smiled or talked. But they had taken everything, and, giggling like schoolboys, had swung him by the arms and legs chorusing "Heave! Heave! Heave!"

According to Beanie he had bounced once on the grading, flipped neatly in the air and made a swan-spread belly-flop right into the Box Elder River. He had stayed right there in the icy, springtime water wading neck deep until he found a clothesline near enough to the water's edge.

Wearing his new clothes, bib-overalls which flapped high on the ankle and a too-small work shirt, he walked toward the center of town, thoughtfully exploring with his tongue the vacancy in the front of his mouth and considering his mistake in believing that the Deity would help him prosper in such an honorable line of work.

But before dark he had a job hashing, pearl-diving and waiting tables in a tiny, narrow restaurant owned by a man named Harris. Harris spent most of his time at the Palace Bar next door, appearing only occasionally, and then to empty the till or to lurch heavily to his rooms above the restaurant. Beanie was left to cook, serve and, after the first month or so, to run the financial end of the business.

From the first day it had been Beanie's plan to rob Harris and run, but there was never quite enough left in the till to get him a decent distance out of town, so Beanie waited, confident that one day the opportunity for big, quick money would present itself. When it did Beanie would be gone.

Then Harris disappeared. For several days he failed to appear at the cash register or at his rooms, and Beanie found that he had not been seen at the Palace Bar. Beanie began to become excited watching the money pile up in the till, and within a month he had his stake.

But with bag packed and the money in his pocket, he hesitated. It was difficult to walk out and leave everything sitting there — food, equipment and a gum-ball machine full of gum balls. He decided to stay until he had used everything up.

After the second month he began to realize that there was no way to plan so everything would run out at the same time. There was always something left over — always too much to just walk out on.

And then the money just kept piling up in the till.

Finally, the third month after Harris's disappearance, Beanie went into the apartment over the restaurant where his missing employer had lived, and he packed everything that didn't fit or didn't work in cardboard boxes and he put these downstairs in the small unused storeroom behind the restaurant. This done he moved into the apartment himself.

The fourth month Beanie hired a waitress full-time, freeing himself to spend all his time cooking, and he bought a secondhand electric sign, an opaque sandwich of plastic with a bulb in the middle. On the sign Beanie himself painted a picture of a steaming bowl of chili, specialty of the house, and the word "Beanies'." It wasn't long before people began to point out that the apostrophe was in the wrong place, but Beanie would explain carefully that he had wanted it that way and that it conveyed a special meaning known only to him.

When people would ask him about the teeth, he would tell them the story of the hoboes and say that the first time he got enough money to replace the plates he would be gone from Easton forever. He had said this so many times and to so many people that the two things, teeth and departure, were inextricably related. It would be impossible for him to get the one without doing the other. But the truth was that Beanie didn't want to leave town at all. He was making more money than he could spend even with his one extravagant trip every week to Loreen's over the Palace Bar. He was a well-known local figure with very good standing in the small community of his street. He was famed for his stories of the Bible-selling days, his tongue pushing the words out the hole in his mouth like marbles. He had been able to hire both a full-time and a part-time waitress, and although they both robbed him constantly, lost him customers with their arrogance, and quit work on the average of once every two months, Beanie had learned to accept this as an unalterable part of business life.

Then one day even this problem disappeared. The girl had come.

She had appeared one afternoon, this girl, wearing a man's blue, collarless jacket with a zipper in the front and leather sleeves. On the front, over the heart, a shadow of darker color showed that a letter, either "C" or "G," had once been there. To Beanie she looked like a little girl bundled up and ready to sing Christmas carols in front of somebody's house. When she took her first breath to speak, Beanie thought she might burst into "Hark the Herald Angels Sing," but instead she asked him for a job, looking at him clear-eyed and expressionless as a cabbage.

Beanie took his eyes from her and began to study his nails. He hated to say no to anybody, and would go to any lengths to avoid it. Although he could not deny that he had a *Waitress Wanted* sign in the window, this girl was not at all what he had in mind. He hoped, however, to have *her* make the decision not to work for him. He didn't want anyone who would drop her apron and run the first time some wino stumbled in from next door.

"You shink you can schtand the whuckin' work?" he had asked, whistling the words evilly from the cavity of his mouth.

She looked around slowly. It was four in the afternoon, and the place was so empty you could hear the neon buzz. "I kinda doubt I'll get worked to death," she said.

"That'sh right," he said, and he scratched idly at his crotch, bending a little at the knees. "Business's shiddy. I can't pay much."

Her shoulders humped a little under her jacket and her hands disappeared into the leather sleeves like turtle's heads. "I'll work the rest of today and all of tomorrow for meals," she said. "We'll talk about pay tomorrow night."

Beanie considered. There was little doubt that she'd stick, and he could get a day and a half's work free while he found somebody else. "Suitsh me," he said. He took off his apron and handed it to her. The leather sleeves didn't come up to take it.

"Supper first," she said.

After a day and a half of surprisingly skillful work she had been able to strike a very good bargain.

Beanie never asked her where she was from, and she'd never volunteered the information. He noted, however, that she worked as if she had no other place to go, and after it was clear that she wasn't going to be queasy about the type of customer that came in, and that she wouldn't run off as soon as she got a letter from home, Beanie raised her wages to the point where she would not quit. He had naturally expected her to steal, and had chopped her initial wages thirty per cent to make up the difference, but she had proved honest — honest and good-natured and clean and neat and efficient.

To Beanie this was suspicious, and it nearly drove him

mad waiting for the terrible trait which would balance out all the others, but the more he watched and waited, the more things he discovered about her which were invaluable. She wasn't, for example, too good-looking like some he'd had. She was a little flat-chested and thin with a narrow, triangular face and the thinnest, most delicate broken nose Beanie had ever seen. She wasn't sexy enough to fill the place with wiseacre lover-boys who sat at the counter in the afternoons doing nothing but drinking coffee and who came in again later at night drunk and obnoxious. With some girls Beanie had found it necessary to keep the lead-filled billy with him most of the time to break up fights. But this new one gave him no trouble at all. She didn't even mind working extra sometimes when the part-time girl was too hung-over to show up on Sunday mornings.

She ate all her meals right there in the kitchen with Beanie, waiting until the place was empty. For Beanie these became the high spots of the day.

"My God!" she'd say, dropping on the stool inside the kitchen door. "I'm ravished! You have a TV dinner you can heat without screwin' it up?"

"Schmart-ash bitsh!" he'd snarl, and toss a piece of steak on the grill.

On the pretext that he needed her to live within call of the place in case the part-time girl got sick or in case things got especially hectic, Beanie moved all of Harris's things from the unused storeroom behind the restaurant and gave them to the Salvation Army in exchange for a bed and mattress. He also made a deal on a used dresser and a chair. He rented her the room at half the price she had been paying for her old room several blocks down the street. He could watch her more carefully when she was closer. Beanie had not yet given up his search for the unrevealed character deformity.

It was Beanie's belief that for the watchful, cataclysmic events could be prepared for. If a man could be observant enough to see the signs of coming disaster, he might be prepared for them. The mail, for example, was an excellent place to watch for such signs. The girl's mail, when she had any, came through the slot in the door along with the bills for the restaurant, and he waited expectantly until, sure enough, one day she began to receive mail from the office of admissions at the college right there in Easton. These letters would come very early in the morning, and Beanie would wait until she came out of her room; then, with great frowns, lip smackings and close myopic readings of the return address, he would hand them to her. She would look briefly and uninterestedly at them, prop them casually some place out in plain sight and leave them there unopened all day.

Finally Beanie could stand it no longer. It was his custom to read newspapers and detective magazines between orders when friends weren't in the kitchen with him, and one evening, late, while he was cooking supper for her, he tossed a newspaper toward her. It was folded to show a picture of policemen in conflict with demonstrating students.

"Don't that make ya shick to your shtumick?" he whistled in disgust.

"Don't it though," she said, and tossed the newspaper back. "It don't take much brains to beat somebody over the head with a stick." Her face was absolutely impassive.

Beanie didn't say anything for a time. "You want gravy or butter on your potatoesh?" he asked finally, not taking his eyes from the chicken in the deep fryer.

"Didn't you make the gravy?" she asked. "I'll take the butter."

Normally he would have given her the gravy anyway, but this time he cut several patties of the good butter with great dignity and placed them on her mashed potatoes. "A lot of the bashturdsh comin' in here," he said.

"Who," she asked, "policemen?"

It was a second before he answered. "No," he said. "College kidsh."

"Oh," she said absently. She took the tongs and turned the chicken-half in the deep fat.

"I'd rather have drunks off the shtreet," he said. "Dumb whuckersh."

"Who, drunks?"

He smacked his lips together a couple of times patiently. "No," he said. "*Coll*-ege kidsh."

"Oh," she said, nodding her head. "Oh, yeah."

"I been grateful of two thingsh," he said loudly, picking the chicken out of the fat with the tongs. "One is that I wasn't born a queer, and the other is that I never been to college."

"Oh, I don't know," she said, behind him. "There's worse things. You could have been a toothless cook."

He turned toward her with a strangled, low whistle, but she was grinning. "Beanie," she said, "I'll tell you all about it if you'll lend me three hundred dollars."

The money was for one quarter's tuition and fees, and Beanie took her down to the bank where he co-signed a note for her. When they came out of the bank it was raining.

"See?" he said, holding out a hand to the rain with a dour expression. "Thish rain's a sign. Good money down the drain. Thish rain meansh somethin'."

"It means it's March," she said. "It means you better carry an umbrella." She popped her own open and handed it toward him, but he looked away scornfully. For Beanie umbrellas were to be seen only in the hands of women and the infirm. He would rather be caught on the street holding a lollipop. On the other hand he was wearing his favorite plaid tie — left over from Harris's things — and a hound's-tooth sport coat he had found at the Salvation Army which bore the label of a top men's store. "I can't hold this thing high enough for you," she said, and, lowering it over her own head she walked out into the rain. Before she had gone a dozen steps he had taken the umbrella from her and held it over both of them.

"Don't go gitt'n schmart-ash now, ya li'l bitsh!" With a quick cough he hocked something out the gap between his teeth which bounced when it hit the wet sidewalk.

The college experience worked a greater change on Beanie than on Alberta herself. He felt his position in the community vastly enhanced by the fact of Alberta's educational elevation. He himself stood with more dignity and self-assurance in her reflected glory. To his cronies in the back room he let it be known that he was "putting The Girl through college," and he received from the community at large the respect which should be accorded to a patron of the academic world.

In his new position even Beanie's appearance changed. He returned one day from the Five and Dime with reading glasses which made him hold his *Police Gazette*s at a more respectable and dignified distance, and which he learned to fold and return to his breast pocket with a measured grace and an expression of regality. Even his attitude toward Alberta changed. Although their daily relationship remained the same, in public, with customers in the place, Bernie began to address her loudly as "Miss Raynes" in a way which deadened the air and caused customers to stop slurping their soup. When a disturbance violated the dignity of the place, Beanie would slowly reach for his glasses and put them on the end of his nose and squint over them at the offending parties. It was a less violent but equally effective equivalent of the lead-filled billy.

Alberta had almost finished one quarter, the spring quarter, but the last week of the term she received a letter from the Dean of Students which not only denied her credit for that term, but also refused her re-admission to Easton College at any time. It had been discovered that she had lied about her age on her application form so that she could live outside the dormitories, and in checking her mailing address school officials had found that she was living in sin with her employer behind the restaurant where she worked.

Beanie had sensed trouble in the letter as soon as it slid through the slot in the door, and he had insisted that it be read to him.

He was stunned. He was anguished. For an entire day he would neither leave the kitchen nor allow any man to enter it. He felt himself torn from his new elevation to be dragged in shame and covered with infamy. The fact that he, the moral protector and spiritual guardian of this girl should be so accused left him totally without words. The second day he began to speak grimly of pulling strings through influential people on whom he had damaging information. The morning of the third day he spoke of making phone calls to every influential state official whose name he could remember, and by the same afternoon he was threatening to phone directly to the offending parties.

For Beanie, everyone at the college from the lowliest custodian to the president himself was implicated. The guilt included the student body and it spread through the alumnae past and present.

Alberta did not even attempt to explain that she didn't want to go back for another quarter anyway — that she was glad to be finished with the whole business. It was clear to her that the moral inequity of the situation was not responsible for Beanie's anguish. Beanie wanted her back in college so that he himself could be reinstated in the social position from which he had been snatched so cruelly. But most disconcerting of all to Alberta was her realization that he was finding a whole new role as the socially wounded, maligned, unjustly accused innocent, and this new role was beginning to provide for him almost as much satisfaction as his old position had.

She determined to end it once and for all time.

Beanie was drinking coffee and muttering. "Whucker!" he whistled.

"Who?" Alberta said.

"Whuckin' Dean."

"Yeah," said Alberta.

"I never touched you, right?" He held up ten unoffending fingers.

"Never," Alberta said.

"It's an insult," Beanie said. "A schlur. A schlur on your womanhood." He tasted the word and found it good. "A schlur," he repeated.

"A slur," Alberta said, "definitely."

"Is that what they teach up there?" Beanie whined with a pious expression. "Schlurs and insults?"

"They can't say those kinds of things about you," Alberta said.

"Damn right they can't," Beanie said. He was pleased finally to have a support. She had until this point withheld feelings of any kind.

"I can't let them insult me and slur me all over the place and get away with it, can I?" she said.

"Hell no," agreed Beanie. "Buncha Commies."

"A slur on you too," Alberta said. "They slurred you too, Beanie."

"Buncha fairysh," Beanie said in a choked voice. He

made a mincing expression and raised one arm to let the wrist dangle limply.

"Yeah," Alberta said.

"I'm gonna call the dirty whucker up," Beanie said, and he made a move toward the pay phone on the wall, waiting to be called back by Alberta.

"No, by God," Alberta said. "*I'm* gonna call." She marched past Beanie to the phone and deposited her dime and dialed the number while Beanie stood looking uncertain. A cool voice answered. "Dean Callister?" she said in an even, clear voice without special emphasis. "This is Alberta Raynes. Fuck you." She held the phone till she heard the click on the other end, then she felt automatically in the coin return and turned back to Beanie. "That'll fix the son-of-a-bitch," she said.

Beanie said not a word. He returned to the kitchen and she did not see him again for several hours.

Although she had done it primarily to release Beanie from the obligation he felt to reinstate himself and her in their former positions, she would not have said that there was no special pleasure in it for her. Especially to have done it in that particular way. The three months of the quarter had been an ordeal for her. It had been a painful and disappointing experience, and she had continued after the first few weeks only to justify the three hundred dollars. It was like the television set she had sent for as a child, a tremendous bargain at four box-tops and fifty cents. She had been more amazed than disappointed to find that it was barely two inches high and that the picture was made by inserting a strip of celluloid film on the side. On the back of the cereal box there had been no word about size. She had vowed then never again to buy anything she couldn't measure beforehand. She did, though, repeatedly, and she thought of this as her special weakness.

II

The first thing Alberta noticed about Chevy when he came into Beanie's was his hair. It would have been very impressive if it had been just an ordinary brown or black, but instead it was the color of gold found in crayon boxes, and it was heavy and ringlety and thick. He and the very tall man he came in with both ordered chili and coffee and then began immediately to argue. Not angry and shouting, but serious. The one with the hair did most of the talking though. Even after his chili came he just let it get cold while he talked, rising half off his stool and swinging his arms around in all directions. The tall one acted like he thought everything his friend said was amusing. He just kept grinning and eating his chili. Once he caught Alberta watching and he winked at her. Not a wise wink, not a leer — but kind of a knowing wink as if he shared something with her.

Alberta busied herself after the tall one caught her looking at them. It was nearly closing time and she was putting the place in order for tomorrow. If she didn't do things on Saturday night, they just wouldn't get done by the other girl who worked Sunday mornings, and Alberta didn't want to take the chance that Beanie and the girl would get in a fight about things being undone. When that happened either Beanie would fire her or the girl would quit, but in either case Alberta would be called in to work on her one day off.

She was bringing fresh boxes of candy, Hershey and Snickers, for the glass cigar case in the front and she heard her own name being used in the argument. It was unmistakable. The one with the hair was using it and was speaking in a very clear voice. Alberta continued past them toward the candy shelf, but she was uncertain about what she should do. When she had first heard her name she had not been able to keep from turning her eyes toward them, and the tall one had been looking at her and he had winked again. Alberta stared right through him as if he were a convenient window and continued putting away the candy. Behind her she heard the voice of the tall one say, "Well, why don't you ask her then?" and Alberta turned toward them again and this time the tall one motioned her to come over.

"You talking to me?" Alberta said with some menace in her voice, and she walked toward them. It was clear that at least the tall one knew who she was.

"Miss Raynes," said the tall one. "I'd like you to meet Chevy Callister."

"Hi," Alberta said cautiously.

"Alberta Raynes?" said the one with the hair. "Alberta *Raynes?*"

"So?" said Alberta.

"*You* are? *You?*" An expression crossed his face like that of people in the comics who are hit over the head with things. In her own mind Alberta rejected a series of possible reactions and selected an expression some place between a smile and a grimace so that she could go either way depending on what happened. But the one with the hair looked as confused as she was. He was searching her face with his eyes as if he was looking for something special, then he clapped his hands together and leaned back on his stool and began to laugh. "Folks," he said, "we've got 'em. We've got 'em by the short ones." He slid off his stool and stood in the aisle between the counter and the booths. "Ladies and gentlemen of the jury," he said, and he clutched an imaginary vest. "Look at this girl. Is it possible that you can imagine her guilty of these charges — charges which I hesitate to name in her presence. Which of you will so much as say the words before this girl, this angel? Which of you would soil her gentle ears . . ."

"Just what the hell is going on?" Alberta said calmly. The one with the hair just stood there clutching his imaginary vest, an arm extended in a wide gesture. He looked at her with a crazy glazed smile. At first she thought that he had a glass eye in his left eye, then she thought it might be his right. Finally she realized that he was very, very drunk.

"Miss Raynes," he said, sliding carefully back on his stool, "I want to assure you that you have nothing to fear. Not even any small thing, because there is absolutely no doubt anywhere near my tidy mind that you'll be safely reinstated and readmitted in school next quarter. There is no doubt." He was grinning the biggest, happiest, sloppiest, most glassy-eyed smile she'd ever seen, and Alberta couldn't held smiling back.

"Well, thanks anyway," she said, "but I don't want to go back anyway."

"Hmm? What?" said the glassy-eyed one as if he hadn't heard.

"I don't *want* to go back," she said again, but he just stared at her as if he didn't understand. "To school, you know?" she said.

He continued to look at her a long time, occasionally licking his lips as if he were deciphering her words one by one. Finally he sat straight up on his stool and ran his hand back through his hair. A severe line appeared between his eyebrows, and Alberta noticed that the glaze was gone from his eyes.

"What do you mean you don't want to go back?" he said.

She let her own smile turn into a dangerous, overtaxed expression. "What do I mean? I mean I'm not gonna . . . *Lis*ten! What do you mean, what do you mean?"

"Listen!" he said, and his eyes were suddenly very clear. "I've spent about the last three days doing nothing else but trying to get the Dean's office to reconsider. I've written *art*icles for the school paper, I've organized letter-writing groups to Senator Woodrow in *Wash*ington. Right now there's a pe*ti*tion circulating . . ." He numbered patiently on his fingers.

"Next time you want to do me a big favor, you check with me first, huh? Make you a bunch more popular."

A look passed over his face as if he might be silently

counting to ten. His hand came up and passed again through his hair. The tall one nudged him with his elbow. "Git 'em, Chevy," he said. "Sic 'em, boy." He seemed pleased with the progress of things and Alberta began to hate him without bounds.

"*Why* don't you want to go back?" the one with the hair said. He leaned up and placed his elbows on the counter solidly as if entrenching himself for a long siege.

"*Look!*" Alberta said. "I don't have to explain to any . . ."

"First," he interrupted, holding up one finger, "you were sufficiently dismayed at being rejected to call the Dean of Students on the telephone and scream obscenities at him! "Second . . ." — up went another finger —

"I did *not* scream," Alberta said firmly.

". . . and these are not acts of a person who doesn't want to get back into school." In spite of being drunk, he was able to talk so rapidly that it was difficult to understand him.

"You couldn't get me back in that place if you gave me back my three hundred dollars and threw in the goddamned Student *Un*ion building to boot. You couldn't . . ."

"Little too tough for you, huh?" he asked. "Pretty difficult, eh?"

"Great!" The tall one elbowed Chevy again. "That's the way to persuade her. Sweet talk. Sweet talk'll do it every time. The great Budweiser-tongued orator."

Chevy appeared not to hear the tall one. "Just tell me why not," he said. "Give me your reasons in clear, lucid . . ."

"Well, first off," Alberta said, leaning across the counter so that her nose was very close to his, "I'd have to leave off living in sin with my employer-lover, you know, and that'd . . ."

"No! No! No! You wouldn't! That's just the point, you . . ." He caught himself. His eyes widened and he began to look closely at her.

"Beanieeeeeee!" Alberta called.

Above the tin plate on the kitchen door, shiny where shoulders bumped through, Beanie's face appeared in the porthole window. He pushed the door open and stood there glowering, wiping his hands on his apron.

"There," Alberta said, "is my lover. Beanie, these two fellas are from the college."

Beanie's eyes opened like window shades going up and he charged toward them. "Lishen, goddammit," he said someplace between a whistle and a roar, "I don't like the idea of you shpreadin' those whuckin' lies up there!" He pointed a quivering finger in the direction of the college.

"What? What? What?" said the one with the hair, looking from Beanie to Alberta and back again.

"Beanie, these guys are tryin' to get me back *in*. They want me to go back."

This stopped Beanie only for a minute. He lifted his glasses from his pocket, put them on, and peered at the two. "She don't wanna git back in," he sneered.

"Who's he?" Chevy asked Alberta. "Who're you?" he asked Beanie.

"I'm her goddamned guardian," Beanie said, drawing himself up. He refolded his glasses and put them away with great dignity.

"'*Guardian!* Guardian! Listen, I didn't know he was your guardian. *No*body does. They don't know that back at school. You could get back in tomorrow with a public apology." He half stood out of his seat and his eyes swung back and forth from one to the other. "Why the hell didn't you tell them he was your guardian?"

"In the first place," she said, "it's none of anybody's damn business, including yours, what Beanie is; and second, I don't like the idea of people going around trying to get me in school when I don't the hell want to go back to school, okay?"

Chevy's mouth moved for a moment as though it were trying to phrase one last objection. Then he gave up. "Really, huh?" He lowered himself slowly back into his seat and his eyes glazed over again.

"Really! Absolutely! Finally!"

"Well, okay," he said with a sad shake of his head. He stared despondently into his half-eaten, cold bowl of chili. "I just wanted you to know that if you want to go back you can."

"I don't want to."

"I just wanted to put the choice back in her hands, folks," he said in a hurt voice. "I just wanted her to know she *could* go back."

"So I know it."

There was a long silence while Chevy looked into his bowl and Alberta glared at him. Deep in his throat Beanie began to work something into spitting position. Finally the tall one spoke.

"Witness the termination of the undergraduate career of Chevy Callister," he intoned, "boy zealot."

Chevy shook his head, still looking into his chili. He started to smile. "Folks," he said, "I think he's right."

The tall one clapped a hand over his heart and began to declaim in a deep, solemn voice. "The last injustice finally righted, and wrong uprooted at last, Mr. Callister cast his weapons into the sea and retired himself to a place apart. But his days were long, and his deeds many."

The one with the hair closed his glassy eyes tight and leaned dangerously back on his stool and laughed again his laugh that sounded as if it came from deep within him and was released under great pressure. Then he leaned against the counter and his head fell forward into a limp bow.

"I apologize," he said. He looked up with a warm, liquid, harmless grin, and for the second time Alberta couldn't help smiling back at him. "I have imposed myself upon you, and I am sorry."

"It's okay," Alberta said.

"Let me make it up to you," he said, and he wagged his head like a puppy. "Lemme take you to a movie. Name the time. You just name the time and I'll be right there."

"Thanks anyway," she said. She felt Beanie's eyes on her and she was suddenly embarrassed. She began to clean the counter of the chili bowls and the coffee cups.

"Please," he said. "Please."

The tall one stood and tried to take Chevy under the arms and pull him to his feet, but he let himself go limp. He laid his chest and the side of his head flat on the counter and looked at her sideways. "Any time at all. Doesn't have to be a movie. Zoo? Picnic? Spring's a great time for picnics. Church? Sunday school?"

"C'mon," said the tall one. "The girl's not interested."

"Oh, Miss Raynes, I beg, implore, beseech, and petition . . ." He clasped his hands together and made a woeful face. Behind the counter Beanie made a move for the billy.

"Out!" he said. "Out!"

The one with the hair looked at him in surprise, then turned back to Alberta, an expression of genuine dismay and injury on his face. He began slowly to leave his seat and lurch toward the door, his shoulders sagging pitifully. Before she had even known she was going to, Alberta had called out to him. "Hey!" she said.

He turned and Beanie lowered the billy.

"Tomorrow's my day off," she said. "How about six-thirty?"

"Great," he said. "Movie?"

Alberta shrugged and continued to wipe the counter with her cloth, not looking at him. She began already to regret it.

"Great!" he said again. "Where do you live?"

"Here, remember? With Beanie."

"Tomorrow at six-thirty. Right!" He and the tall one went out.

"Well, I'll be dipped in shit," Beanie said. He slammed the billy into its place behind the counter and stalked back into the kitchen. Alberta continued to clean the counter. She wondered what he'd be like sober, this Chevy, and she wondered what his hair would feel like.

SUNDAY TOPICS

Mrs. Callister liked to describe her son Chevy's hair by saying it was just like what you see on ancient statues in *Life* magazine. She would hasten to add that she was aware that they didn't really know how to make hair way back in those ancient days — they just made those big round ringlets. But, she would say, that was just the way Chevy's hair really was — thick, so that even as a child, a baby, it had been difficult to comb. And the color — blond-gold, summer and winter. Mrs. Callister had never seen hair like it on either side of the family. She didn't know where it had come from, but she knew that if she had it she wouldn't shave it off.

But her son Chevy had shaved it off, and he had kept it shaved for most of his senior year in high school.

Those had been bad times for Mrs. Callister. Everybody mentioned it and pretended it was just so cute! But she was not easily deceived. She knew what people were thinking. After all this time, four years, Mrs. Perkins next door still occasionally brought it up. "How's your son Chevy?" she would say. "He hasn't shaved his head again, has he?"

But the thing that she regretted most about it was the picture in the high school yearbook. If you curled your finger over the top of his head or covered it with the side of your hand, he was the handsomest boy on any of the pages, but with your hand away, his head was shiny and peaked and bumpy. Even now it gave Mrs. Callister a sinking feeling deep in her stomach every time she thought about it. Especially with that smile. You could never get Chevy to smile for the camera. Just like his father, he always looked grim in photographs. But there on that bald-headed high school graduation picture was the most brilliant dazzling smile anybody had ever seen.

Chevy's hair was back now, of course, and although he didn't seem ever to get it cut, and although he lived away from home in that church, even though Mrs. Callister knew that he didn't even *go* to that church — in spite of these things and in spite of the awful and unaccountable car that he drove, Mrs. Callister joyfully welcomed her son each week to her Sunday dinner table. She welcomed him thinking that *this* Sunday would be different. This Sunday her son and husband would acknowledge one another in a warm and open way. They would talk and laugh as they had not for three years.

Aside from this one thing, this indirectness and formality between the two, Mrs. Callister had everything she could want: a husband she respected and admired and a son she worshipped. When she entered her kitchen each

Sunday she did so for them, and she did so with a kind of trembling eagerness. It was the alchemy of her cooking that brought the family together on Sundays in the first place, and she had a deep, unspoken faith that if a meal of sufficient potency could be cooked it would overcome and dissolve this single problem that marred the perfection of her days. Such a meal would thaw the tongues of her husband and son. During the week Mrs. Callister prepared meals for her husband. On Sundays she created them.

It had begun, this unaccountable wariness between the two of them, when Chevy was still in his first years of high school, and it had continued until three years ago when he had moved to the church. Mr. Callister was always moody and quiet and reserved. He spoke seldom even to Mrs. Callister, but Chevy had always been so friendly and warm and outgoing and happy, talking all the time since he was just a baby — except to his father. But it wasn't that they didn't *talk*, it wasn't that they didn't *like* each other, it was just that they were so maddeningly indirect, so cautious-seeming. Mrs. Callister could not stand it. When she talked to people she came right out and talked. She got to the heart of the situation. She could bear none of this maddening indirectness. Yet her son and her husband spoke to each other as if they had only a few words left and must budget them carefully. They chose words the way she chose tomatoes.

But today! Perhaps today would be different, because today was even more special than usual. Tonight Chevy graduated from college, and during the previous week Mr.

Callister had finally been promoted — he insisted quietly and firmly that it was an appointment — to Dean of Students at the same college. They had waited patiently for five years for old Dean Harper to die, and finally it had come to pass and now Mr. Callister was Dean Callister. The old Dean had worn out no fewer than six other assistant deans of students, but Mr. Callister had persevered and was now rewarded. But as a last, final nastiness, directed at Mrs. Callister from beyond the grave, the senile old man Harper, whom she had hated steadfastly for five long years, had arranged to die so that it was necessary to bury him last Sunday afternoon, thus disrupting her whole week and making it impossible to serve Sunday dinner.

This Sunday would have to be particularly good then since they had missed the Sunday before, and although Mr. Callister had officially been Dean of Students for more than a week, this would also be his celebration dinner. It annoyed Mrs. Callister that she would be unable to surprise him with a real celebration, a celebration with special things — wine, perhaps, and candles and guests who hid in closets — but of course he would have been furious if she had. He didn't like to have fusses made over things. At least that was what he always said. Mrs. Callister knew, however, that everyone secretly enjoyed having fusses made over them, and she never failed to provide as large a fuss as she thought she could get away with.

Today, for example, she had baked a cake, Mr. Callister's favorite kind — a white cake with rich white frosting. It was double-layered and it had CONGRATULATIONS

DEAN ARNOLD CALLISTER carefully written over the white in green trim. The cake lay now in the cupboard where the good china would have been had not the good china been on the table. Beef roast, home-baked rolls, garden-fresh asparagus in Hollandaise sauce were being prepared. The last in spite of Mr. Callister who probably wouldn't like it. He didn't like difficult things. Mrs. Callister would not have denied to anyone that the Hollandaise sauce was for herself.

But regardless of the work Mrs. Callister invested in her cooking, she was more an overseer of her meals than an eater of them. She spent part of the time absently selecting half a plateful and the rest of the time moving it around her plate with her fork so that by the end of the meal it appeared that she had eaten several helpings of everything. Prior to the meal itself, during the cooking of it, she would review in her mind topics for general discussion, and although she was never able to actually introduce and sustain these topics with any real continuity, she was able to give a definition and unity to the whole verbal chaos created by the husband and the son. If she didn't eat much it was because every single bit of her concentration was needed to direct and channel their mutterings and fragmented comments into some semblance of conversation.

One of the topics for this Sunday was to be Mr. Callister's promotion.

"Well," she said when her husband and son were seated and had begun to eat. "It certainly is going to be difficult getting used to living with a Dean of Students." She tilted her head coyly, her fork still untouched beside her plate. "I'll bet you're proud of your father, Chevy. Did you congratulate him yet?"

There was a silence.

"Arnold, did he . . ."

"Well, actually," Mr. Callister said. "You'd have been surprised how excited he got about it." He started to bring his coffee cup to his lips. "No, not really ex*cit*ed. Hysterical might be a better word."

Mrs. Callister decided to pretend that she thought this was a grand family joke, and she laughed gaily, looking from one to the other, ignoring the fact that the father had spoken as if the son were several hundred miles distant and the son had reacted as if he were deaf.

"Made his feelings quite public," Mr. Callister went on. "Wrote an article for the school paper about me and my job. Didn't I mention it?" He smiled good-naturedly at his wife. Mrs. Callister had just picked up her fork, and now she put it down again in order to look more formally pleased.

"Well, I think it's nice," she said. "I really do." She reflected a moment. "Why haven't I seen it?" she asked.

"Haven't you seen it?" Chevy said, surprise and hurt in his voice. "Gee, Mom, I'd have given you a copy, but I thought Dad would."

Mrs. Callister, the seasoned veteran and victim of the Sunday dinner table, bugled a strategic retreat. "Oh," she said, "it's probably too intellectual for me anyway." She picked up her fork again and smiled the smile of a gentle, flower-raising, Sunday-dinner-cooking, obedient, uncomplicated wife and mother. It was a pose favored by her for the security it offered, and the smile that signaled it was a joy to behold. Chevy beheld it now, smiling a smile of his own.

"Dad must have forgotten," he explained.

"I didn't want to embarrass you," Mr. Callister said to his wife in a rather apologetic voice. "It was rather personal."

"A personal message? In the paper? The school newspaper?"

"Yes, it is a little unusual, isn't it?" her husband said.

When Mrs. Callister weighed something in her mind she was not able to keep the effort from showing on her face. Her lips pressed together and her chin took on the puckered texture of a walnut shell. After a moment she said, "How do you mean *unusual*, Arnold?"

When she used her husband's first name it meant that she would admit no nonsense. She had left the happy homemaker behind.

Mr. Callister looked up as if startled to have stirred up such deadly seriousness in his wife. "I just meant," he smiled, "that it seems unusual that a public newspaper be used to evaluate the actions of one's father."

"A marvelous place, however," Chevy said, "to evaluate the actions of Deans of Students."

Both men were speaking to Mrs. Callister, and she looked from one to the other. Then she smiled. "Dear," she said in a new and happy voice, "don't be so *ser*ious! This isn't a conference. Eat, Drink and Be Merry! We're celebrating your promotion!"

"Appointment," Mr. Callister said softly.

"I *mean* appointment, dear."

There were eating sounds. Mrs. Callister began to place items of food on her plate — a slice of beef roast, a dash of whipped potatoes and a neat stack of asparagus which she covered with the Hollandaise sauce. This done she began to regard Chevy's plate with suspicion.

"Did you see the onions, Chevy? Fresh. Fresh this morning from our garden."

"Mother," Chevy said impatiently, "are you under the impression that your voice alone keeps these walls from crashing in on us? You spend all day fixing a great meal. Give a guy a chance to enjoy it, okay?"

He did not look up as he said this, and he did not take an onion. Mrs. Callister's lower lip advanced on her upper lip and held firm on it for a moment. A chin puckered.

"Do you have an ulcer?" she said. "Chevy, do you? "You're drinking a lot of milk lately."

"I drink milk only on Sundays, Mother. I know that the milk in this house is from cartons you open, and it's in glasses washed by your hand. This isn't milk I drink, it's mother-love." He lifted his glass toward her in a toast.

"I wouldn't be a bit surprised if you have one, Chevy." Mrs. Callister said. "How old were you when you got yours, dear?"

"Mmmmm?"

"Your ulcer."

"Twenty-two or three. I really don't remember."

"Twenty-two. Just your age, Chevy," his mother said delightedly.

"About the time he started eating with you, wasn't it?" Chevy asked. "That give you any clues? That tell you anything?"

His mother didn't answer. She straightened her knife carefully beside her plate. "An ulcer," she said after a moment, "is not a thing to make light of. Your father has had an ulcer for a long time, and it's no picnic. No picnic."

"Oh, I don't mean to make light of it at all," Chevy said. "I fully appreciate the strain it must take, the nervous energy, to keep a Victorian mind in balance in a twentieth-century university."

Across the table Mr. Callister fought with a smile for a second, then overcame it. He took another slice of roast beef and began to cut it into exact squares, cutting carefully one way, then crisscrossing the other. "There are pressures," he agreed. "There certainly are pressures involved in being Dean of Students at a twentieth-century university. Quite a jolt on the nervous system, Victorian or otherwise. For example," he continued, without special emphasis, as if relating some unremarkable fact of his everyday life, ". . . here I've only been Dean for a week or so and already I've received an obscene phone call."

"What?" Mrs. Callister put down her fork in alarm. "What? Who?" She was suddenly short of breath. "*An obscene phone call?*"

Chevy continued to eat as if he had not heard, and Mr. Callister looked at him with amusement. "It was that girl Chevy's so interested in. Alberta Raynes. I suppose I should have had her arrested."

"Ohhh," Mrs. Callister made a sound as if she had been hit in the pit of the stomach. "What did you do?" she said. "You mean you did nothing? Arnold, I was reading that you should phone the telephone company right away and let them know. And the police too. It's your duty. Ohhh, Arnold, an obscene phone call!" She sat away from the table for a moment, breathing deeply, then sat back quickly. "Who's Alberta Raynes?" she asked narrowly. She would not let it get out of control again.

There was a silence while the two men decided who should answer.

"She was a student at the college," the father said finally. "I found it necessary to refuse her readmission for next term. Chevy's article in the paper was about that."

"I mentioned," Chevy announced, "that the policy behind the denial of admission was dishonest, archaic, illogical and against the grain of the society upon which it was inflicted."

". . . and he said it in rather high, rhetorical fashion too, I might add," Mr. Callister said. "A most skillful display of irrelevancies."

Mrs. Callister shifted her eyes from one of the men to the other.

"I'm putting a little reply in the paper myself," Mr. Callister said, ". . . tomorrow."

"Oh?" said his wife coldly. She would have said more, but she could think of nothing sufficiently dry and cutting.

"Tomorrow's the last edition of the paper for the term, isn't it?" Chevy said, shaking his head. "Folks," he said, "witness Justice again o'erthrown."

"Dishonest, archaic and illogical," his father said.

"Well, no wonder you refused her admission, Arnold. Ohhh!"

"That's all after the fact, Mother. My point was that you don't refuse people admission or admit them on the basis of their morality unless you're taking applications for a convent or something. For a college you consider only their academic abilities."

"*Chevyyyy*," said his mother. "Is this girl your *friend?*" She drew back in her chair.

"No," Chevy said after a moment.

"An obscene phone call. Ohh!" Mrs. Callister pushed her plate away weakly.

Mr. Callister continued to eat with a full appetite. He was a highly organized and methodical eater, balancing bites of this with bites of that, maintaining rigid and geometrical borders between potatoes and asparagus.

"And that's what your article was about, Chevy? About that girl?" his mother asked. "You were defending that girl?"

"That's right," Chevy said.

For several moments Mrs. Callister's chin puckered, and when she spoke again she spoke sharply. "Well," she said, "I think it's good for Chevy to have some new interests, Arnold, and I don't think you should make fun of him. I remember when you wanted to be a newspaper man too."

"I don't want to be a newspaper man," Chevy said.

"I've always had the utmost respect for newspaper men," she said, as if this might be the fact needed to change his mind. "Don't you, Arnold?"

"Mmmmm."

"Perhaps you didn't know it, Chevy, but your father once wanted to be a newspaper man too, just after *he* graduated from college. Just think . . ."

Mrs. Callister paused while they thought.

". . . and now he's Dean of Students. Isn't that strange?" She was smiling now at her husband. "At that time he didn't know he was going to be a Dean of Students. You couldn't have predicted that, could you, Arnold?"

Her husband pretended that he had not heard.

"Things have a way of turning out, Chevy," Mrs. Callister said, putting down her fork and folding her hands in her lap. She looked gravely across the table at her son. "I don't think it's necessary to worry if you haven't decided yet what you want to do with your life. Things have a way of turning out for the best."

"I'm not worried," Chevy said.

His mother looked at him unsmilingly for a second, hands still in her lap, then she grasped her fork again and began to poke at a piece of roast beef on her plate. "Oh!" she said suddenly, putting down her fork again. "Chevy, have you had your suit cleaned for tonight? I suppose not! Just like you! Well, bring it over here right away and I'll press it. It's too late to have it cleaned now, I suppose. Oh, no! You wear those black gowns, don't you? They cover the whole suit, don't they? And those square hats?" She looked pleased with herself for having remembered.

"I'm not going," Chevy said.

"Not going?"

"No."

"To your own graduation? You're not going to your own graduation?"

"No, I hadn't planned to. It's just a lot of waiting in line."

The temperature in Mrs. Callister's stomach dropped quickly. "Well," she said, "you've just got to," and she looked at her husband. He continued to eat as if he were alone at the table.

"Why?" asked Chevy.

"Well, *Chevyyyy*," she said, and dropped both hands into her lap in a helpless gesture. "I'll bet Abe goes," Mrs. Callister said. "Mrs. Able would see to that. And Daniel too."

"Probably," Chevy said.

The two men continued to eat while she sat, hands folded, and looked from one to the other. It soon began to occur to her that going through the formality of the graduation *was* probably tiring and foolish and pompous. She remembered her husband's graduation, and it seemed to her that it had made her exceedingly weary. Mrs. Callister's stock in her son's wisdom increased.

"Do you have to go, Arnold? To the graduation?" she asked.

"Yes."

"I suppose you'll have to just sit there for the whole time, won't you?" Mrs. Callister made a sad clicking noise in her mouth. During the silence that followed she prepared the second topic of the day.

"Mrs. Able tells me that Abe has found a teaching job for this fall at a university. The University of — where was it? Pennsylvania? Isn't it strange to be given a teaching job at a university at his age?" she marveled. "With only a Bachelor's degree. The same as you, Chevy." She mused about this while with her fork she arranged the cut pieces of roast beef back into the form of the original slice. "That Abe's a go-getter. He certainly is a young man to respect," she said.

"It's a graduate assistantship," Chevy said. "Not a regular teaching job. And they really aren't too hard to get."

"Well, just the same . . ."

"Would you believe that even a non go-getter like me — that *I* have been offered such a thing?"

"Oh, *Chevyyy*," Mrs. Callister said in a low voice, giving him an expression normally reserved for naughty children. "Don't fib," she said.

"Folks," Chevy said, raising his shoulders, "what's the use? How would you like to grow up with Tom Sawyer for your mother?"

Mrs. Callister's expression changed just enough to show that she had succeeded in rising above this remark. "This is also a kind of celebration dinner for you, Chevy," she said, ". . . for your graduation. It's kind of an important week for our family what with promotions and graduations and everything. Spring is such a time of promise," she chattered, ". . . such a time of beginning. Have you ever noticed that things always seem to end and begin with the spring? School, for example. It always ends in the spring."

"You noticed that too, huh?" Chevy asked, his mouth full. "These modern mothers. Nothing gets past 'em."

"But graduation isn't really an ending so much as a beginning, is it?" Mrs. Callister continued in a vague, reflective way, ignoring her son. "Yes," she affirmed, nodding at her own wisdom. ". . . it's more a beginning."

She let a suggestive silence hang in the air, inviting comment. None was offered.

"And so many things to begin. So much to do for young people today. For people with a Bachelor's degree the horizons are unlimited. So many opportunities and everything. It must be wonderful."

"You have no idea," Chevy said. "It just numbs the mind. The opportunities and everything. It just kind of paralyzes a guy."

Mrs. Callister considered this for a moment. "Yes," she concluded. "The ability to choose, to discriminate. That's a remarkable and an enviable ability." Mrs. Callister pictured in her mind a person with this ability, and she covered her face with a look of distant admiration. "I certainly do respect people who have it," she said.

"Yeah!" Chevy said. "Me too."

"It's such a pity, such a waste when a person is forced to choose in desperation at the last moment because they did not have the ability to choose earlier." Mrs. Callister was speaking more rapidly now and with something like determination in her voice.

"That's right," Chevy said, interrupting the action of his fork to consider this. "I'd never do that. I'd never choose in desperation like that."

"I'm glad to hear you say that, Chevy."

"It'd be better not to choose at all, don't you think?" Chevy continued. "I think what I'd do is just not choose at all."

Mrs. Callister tightened her lips and picked up her fork. She stabbed one of the pieces of reassembled roast beef and placed it in her mouth, chewing with short, quick movements of the jaw, tasting nothing.

"Sure is nice to get a home-cooked meal like this," Chevy said suddenly. He leaned back in his chair to show an empty plate. "That was really a meal," he said. He patted his stomach. "Really a meal."

"Wasn't it though?" his father agreed. "What would be good now would be a piece of white cake. I haven't had a piece of white cake for a long time."

"Wouldn't that be good though?" Chevy said.

Mrs. Callister smiled and there was a sudden color in her cheeks. "You'll never guess what," she said.

THE LEAKPROOF SMILE

Chevy had been out of bed for almost an hour that morning before he remembered about the date he had made with Alberta Raynes. He stopped stock-still for several long seconds, and when he began to move again he had made up his mind to forget the whole thing.

For Chevy this was almost impossible. If somebody asked aloud in his presence, just conversationally, what was the name of Don Quixote's horse, or who played second for the Indians when Al Rosen was playing third — if somebody made the mistake of wondering how much a gallon of water might weigh on the moon, Chevy's eyes would glaze over and he would be lost until he had the answer. He was perfectly aware that the answers were not the real object of the search. When he'd been young he'd done it for the same reason other kids had thrown tantrums, and somehow it had become a habit, though it wasn't really a bad one. It came in handy in many ways. But when Chevy became aware that he was momentarily unable to remember something, his mind would react just as it did to questions.

Before he could forget about Alberta Raynes, then, his mind had locked on the problem of exactly what it was that must be forgotten, and now he couldn't make it stop remembering.

The events which had taken place at the chili parlor were very vague, but it seemed that the girl had agreed to go to a movie, but only after he'd badgered her for a while and generally created a scene. She must have known, he reasoned, that he was drunk, and she probably didn't expect him to show up anyway. If he actually appeared she'd probably just make some excuse. It was really the best thing to just forget about it.

But Chevy winced a little at the hazy memory. If he remembered correctly he'd almost been thrown out of the place.

But the girl herself . . .

He probably wouldn't have given her a second glance under normal circumstances. His preference ran to darkness and to heaviness of lips and hair and breasts. The girl, his mind told him after a little while, was slight and fair with green eyes and short mink-colored hair which fit her head like an over-large German helmet. And to make her even less attractive, she was young. Even before his mind had begun the reconstruction he'd remembered clearly about the youngness. It had been one of the strongest impressions he'd had.

But the face. The eyes were the dominant feature, more round than almond-shaped. They were huge and they should have been brown and moist — doe-like — but instead they were green and clear. When Chevy thought about the eyes two images came to mind. The first was the happy, over-bright eyes of damaged, sickly Tiny Tim, and the second was of the trusting cartoon bear, obligingly sitting on the powder keg.

It was certain, though, in either case, that in the scheme of her face the eyes dominated all. At first those green, cartoon-bear eyes seemed filled with nothing more than an idiot innocence, but then he recalled that the flesh deepened in color both over and under them, and this darkness greatly modified the innocence and produced an impression of placid, confident knowledge — knowledge secure, but won at some expense. The rest of the face continued this pattern of opposition begun by the innocent eyes with their modifying shadows. There were freckles which spread from cheekbone to cheekbone across the nose, and the nose itself, clean-lined like a model's, delicate and fragile, was broken at the joint of cartilage and bone. It wasn't crushed or disfigured; it angled off in an even, neat bend which might have been laid out with draftsman's tools.

By the time Chevy left the church for his parent's house and dinner that afternoon, the face stood with photographic clarity in his mind — the features decorated with a kind of tilted, impish grin, and Chevy knew that he would have to see her in the flesh. She had, he reasoned, regardless of the circumstances under which she did it, agreed to go to a movie with him, and since he had committed himself, he would honor the date.

He planned that he would arrive a few minutes early at the chili parlor, time for a cup of coffee while he studied her and made comparisons between her and his memory of her. If she was what his memory had produced for him — if she was anything vaguely like it, then she'd take some close examination.

There was a parking spot directly in front of Beanie's, and Chevy pulled into it, but before he was entirely out of the car he heard the aluminum screen of the place slam and he saw the girl walking toward him.

"Hi," she said.

He saw that she was wearing a skirt and a sleeveless sweater of unrememberable color, and that she wore sunglasses which covered her from eyebrows to cheekbones and wrapped around toward her ears like goggles. His heart sank. The eyes were hidden. She went directly to the rider's side of the car and began pulling at the door handle.

"Have to come around and get in on this side," Chevy said.

She gave the door a couple more shakes. "What'd you do," she asked. "Weld it?"

"Yeah," Chevy said. "You'll have to come around to this side."

She had started toward him, then returned to the door for one last shake and a closer examination of the weld spots, touching them with her fingers to establish their authenticity. "Welded, huh?" she said.

"Yeah," he said, and he posed grandly, hamming it to the limit, providing for her an introduction to character, an easeful humorous mood and an easy avenue into conversation. "It kept rattling and popping open all the time," he said.

Somehow she missed it. "Well now," she said. "How about that?"

Without looking at him she ducked under his arm as he held the driver's side door and slid across the seat. Chevy closed his eyes in momentary pain before he followed her. Things did not augur well.

"What kind of a car is this, anyway?" she asked when they were both established.

"Henry J," he said, and for the first time since he'd owned the car he found himself wishing that it was a Volkswagen or a Ford. For the first time he felt like a poseur.

When she heard the make she reached up and rapped on the dash with her knuckles, then nodded in satisfaction. "Sure is," she said.

"Oh, boy," Chevy said to himself. "Oh boy, oh boy, oh boy!"

The movie which she wanted to see followed the exploits of a great, black stallion, wild and friendless except for a ten-year-old boy. Chevy watched the screen only when the music rose to a pitch that could not be ignored. Alberta's face, though he could see only the profile, was far more interesting. It covered a range of expressions and emotions which exceeded, all by itself, the efforts of the entire cast of the movie. She ate popcorn, dredging handfuls from the sack and stuffing them wholesale into her mouth, her eyes never leaving the screen; and when something momentous seemed imminent she would suspend the motion, the overloaded hand frozen between the sack and the partially open mouth; then, the crisis resolved, the hand would continue. During the course of the movie he replaced the original bag twice.

The house was packed with whistling, shouting candy-throwers. Chevy and Alberta were sitting on the aisle, and three boys were sitting inside the aisle from them. A dozen times before the cartoon and newsreel were over, one or another of the three would demand exit, and each time Chevy would half-stand, folding back his seat to make room. Finally Chevy caught one of them as he started to slide by and hissed in as dangerous a voice as he could produce to get the hell back to his seat and sit down and stay there. The boy stared almost politely but without expression, letting his arm hang limply in Chevy's grasp. When he was released he continued out into the aisle as planned. Chevy glanced out of the corner of his eye at Alberta and he thought he heard her snicker.

After Chevy had adequately explored Alberta's profile, the palms of his hands and the contents of his wallet, he began desperately to want a cigarette. Once, when he was looking back toward the projector, he had noticed a tint of blue in the dusty cone of light, and, given courage by this, he leaned forward and tried to light up. The brilliant flare of the match startled even him, and the usher appeared almost immediately, his face working in a wordless reprimand and his unlit flashlight waving. On the other side of Alberta the three boys giggled. Chevy hunched down and put his knees up on the seat in front of him and began to consider what would be the proper path for the rest of the evening. After those first bad moments in the car he'd been ready to call it off as quickly as possible, but now, with time to reflect and time to have seen her face, he was beginning to hope that it was just a misunderstanding — something that could easily be straightened out.

Sitting there with his knees drawn up Chevy began to become very excited about the girl again. He'd been very close with the face. Very close. There really were freckles and the eyes were really green and large and deep and ringed with dark. And the incredible pattern of contrast actually was there. But the most amazing thing was that his memory had only scratched the surface. When he'd been able to look into those eyes for the first time after she'd taken off her sunglasses, his impression was that these eyes betrayed not only innocence, but a vulnerability, a breakability, a perviousness that was difficult for him to look at without flinching. And even this was immediately contradicted by the darkness which gave her more than anything else a look of dogged durability. It was the same with the freckles and the broken nose. The nose itself was broken, but not damaged, somehow. Looking at it Chevy suspected that the girl had not lost the fight in which the neat bend had been acquired.

Sitting there, trying to analyze his feelings about her, trying to understand why he felt as strongly and as positively about her as he did, Chevy decided that there was something eminently worthy-seeming and honest and uncompromised about her.

He squirmed a little lower in the seat and crossed his arms over his chest. It was the vulnerability and fragility that disturbed him. These were very probably the things that had made her tense and insecure enough to miss the bit about the welded doors and the Henry J. That was undoubtedly it. She was probably even a virgin.

The skin tightened around Chevy's eyes and a furrow appeared between his brows while he thought about it. His jaw muscles began to work. The first thing he must do would be to rid her of that encumbrance. He must seduce her, and the sooner the better. For her own good.

When they left the theater his intention had been to just drive around until he knew enough about her to form a good plan for seduction, but the girl, still under the spell of the movie, had begun immediately to talk about horses and simply could not be diverted from the subject and into his prepared topics. It turned out that she not only liked horses inordinately, but had actually thought that she was a horse until she was thirteen years old. It was the greatest trauma of her life, she said, when she discovered that she could not, no matter how hard she tried and practiced, be anything but a girl.

Although the moon was very bright, it was impossible in the car to see her face clearly, and at first Chevy thought that he was in the presence of someone with a very highly developed sense of self-satire. At first he had grinned and nodded and met her words with a flood of over-ripe enthusiasm, but her voice continued to come to him full of sincerity and without a trace of humor. She had collected pictures and figurines of horses, she said, and had learned to draw and carve horses. She'd read horse books by the thousands and somewhere even now at home (she pointed a thumb west) were boxes and manila folders bulging with carvings, pictures and books. She scrambled to her knees on the seat and produced from her purse a magazine-torn picture of a horse called Man-O'-War and held it in front of his eyes as he drove, pointing out special features of excellence. This done she settled back in the seat and began somewhere in the middle of the history of the man-horse relationship and worked both ways.

Chevy was amused by all this and even a little interested, but it was taking him no nearer to his intended object. He stopped driving aimlessly and headed toward the church. When he was in the parking lot adjacent to it she had still shown no signs of exhausting her subject.

Chevy's church was a massive stone structure in the old style, its builders having thought of it as a symbol of man's permanence and the durability of his faith. In the glaring moonlight it crouched heavily on the earth, squat and sullen. Although a tall lightning-rod-tipped spire pierced the air above, the building had always seemed to Chevy not to reach up but rather to burrow. It appeared to have succeeded in burying its greater part under the surface like an iceberg.

Chevy had some prepared words on the subject of this and other churches and of church architecture generally, but he was given no chance to speak. The girl continued her lecture as they left the car, seeming not to notice at all where she was. She followed at Chevy's side as he walked around to the side of the building and to the heavy iron-hinged door. Chevy produced a key and opened the door, and at this point she became aware of where she was. Her eyes opened wide and she tensed visibly, but she said nothing.

"My place," Chevy said. "I live here." He bet himself that she wouldn't comment on this and was pleased to find that he was right. She followed wordlessly while he led her in and through the darkness of deep, heavily polished wood and between rows of quiet, dark pews lit strangely by the strong moon through the high, bullet-shaped windows. Above and ahead of them as they walked loomed the choir loft with its massive organ — the pipes shining dully like artillery shells for some awesome and unknown weapon.

Chevy and Alberta walked up a set of carpeted stairs, past the organ and through another small door. Once inside Chevy snapped on lights.

"My God," she said. "You do!"

"Hmmmmm?" he said with some pleasure.

"Do live here. In a church!" She began to inspect things, laying her hands on them.

The room was dominated by two objects. The first was the sagging bed which occupied a large part of the room, and the other was a massive sheet of black canvas which covered an area of one wall. It reached high toward the ceiling. Seeing the canvas it was realized that there were no windows in the room other than the one it covered. There was a desk and book, a typewriter and a half-eaten plate of spaghetti with a cigarette neatly centered in the middle. Above the desk were pictures and torn, red-underscored pages from journals and magazines and scrawled messages as high as the arm could reach. There was a couch, blanket-covered, and an easy chair with a punctured, airless seat and fat beefy arms. There was a rusty and ash-ground rug. In one corner stood a large, open, dish-filled porcelain sink, and next to it sat a hot-plate on a spindly, temporary-looking stand.

Alberta made her way around the room, testing with her finger tips, peering. Finally she sat on the edge of the bed and bounced tentatively. She looked up at him, obviously trying to phrase the question, but Chevy didn't wait for it.

"Custodian and watchman," he explained. "Repairman and handyman. Gardener and pew-polisher *par excellence.*" He dropped into the easy chair and sprawled happily. "But most of all," he said, "I'm a professional backslider, having perfected the gentle art of convincing the Reverend Billy D. Havescold and his Council of Elders that I am restrained from a total commitment to the forces of evil and darkness only by the purifying influence of occasional discussions with the good Billy D., and by the very cleansing nature of my life and work within these stone walls."

Alberta listened attentively to all this, somehow managing not to see the gestures and expressions which were to have indicated the playfulness and lightness of the words.

She thought for a moment. "How long?" she asked seriously.

"Three years."

She pointed to the black canvas. "Stained glass?" she asked. She made a high, bullet shape with her hands.

He nodded. "They ask me to keep it covered at night. Light in a church at night is sinister. Makes people think of monks with candles. Secret passages and all that Gothic stuff."

"This isn't *too* hard to believe." She bounced again on the edge of the bed. "They pay you too?"

"Lavishly."

"Man!" she said, and she began to look around again in wonder.

"Well," Chevy said. He was anxious to get on with it. "What do you like besides horses?" It had, even to his own ears, a very synthetic ring.

"I was boring you, huh?" she said, looking straight at him.

"No!" he said. "Not at all!" and he made enthusiastic motions with his hands to show his boundless interest in horses, wishing that she'd begin to talk — yield up a little information about herself. As it stood he didn't have the slightest idea which flank to approach this girl on. She had not yet revealed the proper vulnerability. She had not yet revealed anything at all.

"Where're you from?" he said. "What's your father do?"

"Chong," the girl said in a soft voice, and she tilted her head and closed one eye and sighted at him as if over a rifle.

"What?" he said.

"Well," she said. "It'd be impressive if I could tell you that I came from a broken home and endured poverty—rickets and rats in the cradle and all that . . ." She smiled and tried to look enthusiastic, but the energy she had brought into the room and the interest with which she had handled things was definitely on the decline. "Bore you worse'n the horses," she said. "Normal amount of mothers and fathers. Oh!" It was like an afterthought. "One brother." She looked like she didn't have another word to say.

"Hmmm," he said with great interest. "Well, how'd you wind up in Easton?"

She shrugged. "Where the money ran out," she said.

"Really?" he said, and he waited for her to continue. This was the kind of information he needed. She stared at him wordlessly, however, and he, not knowing what else to do, stared wordlessly back. Then her mouth suddenly began to curve into a bright, desperately gay smile he hadn't seen on her or on anybody before. The lips swooped in a deep up-pointed curve but stayed pressed together as if the mouth was full of something that might leak, and the sight of it drove from Chevy's mind the next question he had prepared. They continued to stare at each other a long moment, smiling, then she took a deep breath and clapped her hands together and bounced once on the bed.

"Well," she said. "Beautiful spring day."

"Certainly was," Chevy agreed, clearing his throat.

"I just love spring. I think it's my favorite time of the

year," she proclaimed. It came out of her in a burst of joy.

"It certainly is nice." In his mind the prepared topics fluttered away like dry leaves. Chevy began to plot a way to end the evening as soon as possible. Get her the hell out of his room. With one hand he began to massage the side of his head. He squinted his eyes and wrinkled his forehead, the deep ditch appearing between his eyebrows.

"By the way," the girl said. "I hope you didn't think that I was ungrateful last night. I really appreciate all your efforts to help me get back in school."

Hope flickered. "That's all right," Chevy said. "Still don't want to go back?"

"I'm afraid I'm not ready for college." She looked down at her hands, folded neatly in her lap. "I believe that I have some more maturing to do before I go back again."

Chevy searched her face to see if there was the tiniest twinkle in her eyes. There was not. He ran his hand through his hair and ground his teeth together inside compressed, smiling lips. Oh Jesus! Sweet Jesus! he said to himself.

"Someday I'll go back," she continued, "but not right now. I think everyone should have a college education though, don't you?"

"Education's a great gift," he said, "truly."

"Oh, yes," she said. "I'm just not old enough to appreciate it now. I'll go back again when I'm — you know . . ."

"More mature?" offered Chevy. He began to massage his temples again, this time with a vigor that could not be ignored.

"Yes," she said. "More mature." She was silent, and he could tell that she was watching him. "Is something the matter?" she asked eventually.

"Matter?" Chevy said, lifting toward her a face as full of pain and misery as he could manage.

"With your head?" She tapped her own head.

"It's nothing," Chevy said with a weak smile. "Migraine."

"Oh, I'm sorry."

Chevy left an eloquent painful silence in the air while he continued to rub the side of his head. He wondered how fast migraines could develop.

"What are you?" she asked suddenly.

"What *am* I?"

"I mean in school?"

Chevy shook his watch out of his sleeve. "Right at this moment I should be graduating. Yes, right along about now."

"How fabulous," she said, and she tossed one of her hands gaily into the air. The leakproof smile appeared, and it was clear to Chevy that headaches cut no ice with this girl. There seemed no alternative but to be more direct, and Chevy loosened his hold on his tongue.

"Well," he said. "Hasn't it been just a *won*derful evening? Just *fab*ulous? My only regret is that I wasn't able to find a Doris Day movie for you."

She raised her eyebrows and looked uncertain.

"Certainly you like Doris Day," he said. "I mean, I just assumed . . ."

"She isn't exactly my favorite," the girl said guardedly.

"Really?" Chevy asked.

She searched his face, but he had covered it with a bright, up-pointed smile.

"Well," he said, "I'm just certain that you like musical comedies." He tossed one of his hands up gaily. "With all that singing and dancing, I'll bet you just *love* it. Like spring, I'll bet."

She didn't answer. Her smile slowly flattened itself out.

"If it wasn't so late," Chevy said, "we could top the whole wonderful evening off with a nice trip to the basement of the Five and Dime. They've got a couple of new rides down there. They've got a fire engine that goes 'ding' and a stagecoach . . ." He dazzled her with the leakproof smile. ". . . or aren't you mature enough?"

"Listen, you son-of-a-bitch," she said. "You started this whole . . ."

"*Me!*" Chevy came out of his chair toward her. "What was I sup . . ."

". . . started this whole goddamned . . ." She shook a pistol finger at him.

"You came on with all that . . ."

". . . what's your *faaaa*ther do? Where you *from?* What . . ."

"What was I supposed to do? What else can you say to somebody who starts to talk about maturity and . . ."

"But *first* you were . . ."

"Folks!" He turned so that his back was toward her and his appeal was pitched suddenly to a very low, controlled key. "Didn't I think at first that this was one of the rare ones? One with the courage to be different? Was it my fault that she turned out to be just another of those little girls, those charming children who fluff and prance and giggle?" He turned back to her and saw her eyes become even larger. The greenness in them seemed for a moment to be electric.

"Well you . . . Well I . . . Well what was I supposed to do when you . . ."

"Oh, Alberta," he said, and he lifted a silencing hand toward her, amazed at himself. He had found an entry into it and all that was necessary now was to relax and flow into the pattern — just let the words come of their own accord. Inwardly he exulted. He was going to nail this stupid bitch. "I'm sorry," he said. "I really am. It's true that I had no right to expect anything unique from you. I'm sorry. I'll just never get used to the idea that people are just people, no more, no less. Just people."

He met her eyes again for a moment and he thought he saw her body coil into itself. For just an instant he thought she might leap from the bed and land snarling on his shoulders. She began to say something, then either changed her mind or discovered she couldn't.

"I'm sure you have as much honesty and tolerance and courage as the next person," Chevy continued. "It's just that I've been looking for somebody very special for a long time, and I had just about given up hope. When I met you last night I thought . . ." He waved one of his hands with a little hopeless gesture. ". . . but no matter," he said. He returned to the stuffed, airless chair with slow sad steps.

Again she started to say something and again changed

her mind before she had uttered a word. Instead, the light just died in her eyes. It was as if she had, with some hidden switch, turned off both a hearing aid and the lights. She pulled her mouth to the side in a bored expression.

"At first," Chevy continued, "I thought you were a highly original person — someone with strong mind and will, and then you started all that crap about maturity and I got disappointed and lost my temper. I'm really very sorry. I had no right to expect such things from you. I have no right . . ." he said, looking at the floor, ". . . to expect them from anybody." He sighed. "I don't know why I always do."

He had expected some answer, but she had covered her face with the expression used by proper ladies in crowded elevators.

"I mean I don't know what you *are*, Alberta! You keep showing me things you think I'd like to see, and you wait for me to choose one. Show me what you *are*, Alberta! Just show me that! Do you *know* what you are?" Chevy appeared to be very moved by this part of his speech, and he buried one hand in his hair and covered his eyes briefly with the other one. "Do you know what *I* am?" he asked in a tremulous voice. "Do you *care?* Nobody! Nobody understands anybody else. Nobody knows anybody else because nobody is honest with either themselves or other people."

He began to crisscross the room with quick, nervous strides. His voice had become rapid and impassioned.

"When I first met you, Alberta, I thought you might be the one — the one in a billion. All the signs indicated it. The woman I've been looking for. For a whole day I let myself . . ." Chevy's voice caught, and he started over. ". . . let myself hope that it might be you. And now I'm telling you about my feelings. I'm being honest and open. That makes me vulnerable."

He thought it might be a good idea at this point to tear open his shirt and expose his flesh to her, but at the last moment he decided against it.

"Let me tell you what I want," he said, and he began to pace again, feeling exceptionally fine and easy and although she had, as nearly as he could tell, made herself both blind and deaf, the words continued to come well.

"What I want is a relationship with a woman which does not have its back broken by guilts before it begins — which is not built on deception. I want no games and no pettiness and no role-playing. Total personal and total sexual freedom. No inhibitions or restraints or guilt or shame. Maybe it's not possible at all, but goddammit I want a chance to try." He stood for a moment motionless in the center of the room, waiting for a reaction, but there was none. She sat unimpressed and unruffled, looking neither at him nor away.

"That's why I was disappointed," he said. "And that's why I said unkind things. Because for nearly a whole day I felt — more deeply and strongly than ever before — that I had found someone. I thought, Alberta, that it might be you."

He could hardly believe it, but he heard her voice and felt her eyes full and direct. "How did you expect to find out if it really was me?" she asked.

He ran a hand through his hair and placed a look of sincerity on his face. Within him a victory chant began.

"I'd *know*," he said. "I couldn't help but know. There would be an instant recognition between us. The woman would have wanted the same things too — these freedoms, and she would have seen in my eyes that I was the same. Alberta," he said, "I saw that recognition in your eyes. I did." He could easily have held forth longer on the subject, but she spoke again.

"What did you plan to do if it was?" Both her questions were characterized by a lack of emphasis.

"Ohhhh," he said, coming very near to her. "There would be such a joy. There could be no alternative to a physical celebration between us. A total meeting of the spirit and the flesh. There would be so many things to say. So many things to do. I'd want . . ." he said tremulously, watching her eyes carefully, ". . . I'd want to make love like nobody has ever made love before."

She began to inspect his face carefully, and in her own face, in those vulnerable eyes, he thought he saw an uncertainty.

"In the restaurant," he said, "last night, I knew immediately that I felt something flow between us, and I thought I noticed something in your eyes. I thought — I thought that I read something there especially for me. Something only I could read. Something that said we were the same. The same."

"Are you making all this up?" she asked, and although she tried not to show it, the uncertainty came out into the open.

"It's an insult," Chevy said in a low voice, drawing himself up, "to suggest that I am not telling the truth — that I am not being honest with you."

She continued to look at him and he saw the uncertainty change, harden into something else that he couldn't name. As he watched she stood and without warning began to pull the sleeveless sweater over her head. When it was off she reached behind her for the hooks on her brassiere.

"What are you doing?" Chevy asked as calmly as possible. He didn't quite believe that it was happening.

"I want to have a total meeting of the spirit and the flesh," she said brightly, and she tossed the brassiere to the top of his dresser. "I want to be made love to like nobody's ever been made love to before."

"If this is a joke," he said unevenly, "then it's a pretty damn bad . . ."

"It's no joke," she said. She had been unzipping her skirt, but now she stopped and looked at him, the uncertainty returning. "Unless you were joking."

"No, of course not. I wasn't . . ."

"Then I'm not. I'm just trying to be honest." She continued with the skirt. "I'd like very much to try for the kind of relationship you were talking about."

"Now?"

"Without inhibitions or restraints or guilt or shame," she said.

Chevy walked to the chair and sat and crossed his legs. He began to examine something on the palm of his left hand. A line appeared between his eyebrows. "Are you certain you've considered this adequately?" he asked. "I mean this is kind of a big . . ."

"I've always wanted that kind of thing — like you talked about," she said.

"Really?" he said. It was a little voice.

"Really." She stepped out of her panties, hooked a toe in them and flipped them up neatly so that she could catch them. She dropped them on the floor near the head of the bed, and all the time she was speaking, growing more and more excited. ". . . and if we could do it. If we really could do it . . ." She leaped stiff-legged several times on the rug as if practicing for a sack race, grinning hugely at him, ". . . wouldn't it be great?" She jumped on the bed and tucked her feet under her. "Hurry up!" she said.

"Look," Chevy said, and he cleared his throat. "These things take some preparing for. I'm not certain if I'm prepared to . . ."

"Don't worry about that stuff," she said. "My period's just over, so it's okay. I'm probably sterile as a donkey anyway."

"No, I mean . . ." He cleared his throat again and the inside of his mind began to get dark. After a moment he stood and began to undress.

He found himself suddenly ungainly and awkward and he felt irregularly formed. With one foot raised to remove his trousers he lost his balance and went lurching off like some wounded, graceless animal toward the dresser to regain his footing. She chuckled and he answered with a tight, red, joyless smile. Naked, he started belligerently toward the bed.

"Hold it!" she commanded.

Not knowing what else to do, he held it.

"Attennnn-*hut!*" she said. "Leeeeft *face!* Riiiiight *face!* Abouuuuuut *face!* Abouuuuut *face!* Presennnnnnt *arms!*"

ROTC-trained for such emergencies, Chevy wheeled

and turned until she began to chuckle again, rolling back on the bed and holding her stomach.

"I don't see what's so damn *fun*ny about all this," he said when he could speak.

She tried to sober her face. "I'm sorry," she said, but he could tell that she was not.

"I thought I'd made it abundantly clear that I considered this a serious matter." He walked toward the dresser and steadied himself there.

"I thought you said something about a celebration," she said. He looked sharply at her, but her face was clean of expression.

"I said *physical* celebration," he said. "I didn't mean with horns and funny hats."

Somehow, without clothes, facial expressions failed and sarcasm was drained of its sting. His right arm leaned on the dresser, but his left arm and both legs felt newly acquired and imperfectly mastered.

They stared at each other for a moment.

"I didn't think this would all be so awkward," she said.

"*Who* is?" he said. His mind had been elsewhere.

"Who is *what?*"

"*Who*'s awkward?"

"This is," she said, and she gestured vaguely between them. "I just didn't think that it would be." There was something in her voice that he didn't know, that he hadn't encountered yet.

"Of *course* it's awkward," he said. "Of *course!*"

"Chong," said Alberta, and she began to look sadly at her hands.

"What do you expect?" he said. "It would be a simple

matter for me just to *couple* with you if that's all you want." He had hit the word "couple" a little too hard, and it rattled around the room with an artificial, tinny sound. Chevy saw that it would be necessary to continue talking until he had drowned the memory of it in other words.

"We'll both have to learn to yield," he said quickly, "but we'll both have to do it equally. No special concessions to your femininity or to my masculinity. From this moment forward we'll abolish the very distinction. We're just two people who want to know the other one thoroughly and to be known thoroughly by the other person. We should help each other to find both an ultimate sexual and an ultimate personal experience and try to sustain them."

"Hooray," said Alberta, throwing up her hands. "Hear! Hear!" she said.

"God*damn* it!" Chevy said. "Will you please the hell be serious?"

"I'm *ser*ious!" she said. "*Je*sus! Just because I don't have some big wrinkle between my eyes doesn't mean I'm not . . ."

"You're not serious," he said. "You're afraid to be serious."

"Can't a person be happy serious?" she asked. "I'm *happy* serious."

They stared at each other across the room until it was seen that neither would be the first to lower their eyes. When this was established they arranged to look away at the same time.

The inside of Chevy's mind threatened to go dark again.

There was a package of cigarettes on top of the dresser, its edge just peeking out from under the brassiere she had thrown. He took them and, holding them firmly for ballast, turned his back on her and ventured across the room to his fat-armed chair. He expected that by the time he turned around she would be up and in the process of dressing herself. His plan was that he would sit, calmly smoking until she finished, then rise and, still naked, politely hold the door for her as she left. But when he turned around again she was still sitting naked on the bed and still staring at her hands. Chevy turned his own eyes to the filter on his cigarette, looking at it as if it had just insulted him.

Finally the silence became too oppressive. "Look!" he said a little desperately. "I mean we're both in unfamiliar territory here. I mean we can't just make up our minds to have this kind of relationship and then just *have* it. We've got to get *used* to each other. Don't you think so?"

She nodded, still looking at her hands.

"There's got to be time to establish a *per*sonal basis. There has to be a *per*sonal basis for a satisfactory sexual act. We've got to get to *know* each other."

"Why?" she asked, as if she really wanted to know.

"Well . . ." he said. "Ahh, well, I mean there are things we each need — special things which the other one must know about, and . . ."

"Special?"

"Yes, personal things."

"Well," she said uncertainly, "is there something, you know, *special* you want me to do?"

"Special?" he asked, baffled.

"I mean is everything *okay* with you?"

He stared at her for a moment while her meaning became clear, then a high color entered his cheeks while the area around his mouth turned a gray-white. "Listen," he said tersely, "I have screwed more women . . ." A sufficient comparison eluded him.

"I'm sorry," she said. "I didn't mean . . ."

"I mean, *Christ*," he said. "We were trying to do this thing without the usual sacred processes. At least I am." He discovered that the use of his arms had returned to him and he gestured experimentally. "One of the sacred assumptions of sex is the male-aggressor bit. You've been sitting there casually assuming that it's my duty to make a special series of goddamned moves, and when I didn't, you make the assumption . . ."

"I'm sorry," she said. "Really, I didn't mean . . ."

"It doesn't matter what you *meant* to do. Only what you *did* do, dammit!" He was deliriously happy to find that suddenly his limbs were useful and he was suddenly at ease again. "Now look, Alberta, don't you see that our society brings us up with certain ideas about things like sex, and don't you see that those ideas are rooted? I mean they're in there for good, and we can decide in our minds that they're wrong, but our impulses are all screaming to us to act by them anyway, do you see?"

Alberta's face showed her to be puzzled. She screwed a finger earnestly into one ear as if searching for the trouble there.

"It's damned hard work to act contrary to those impulses," he continued. "I mean society teaches us to act in a certain way. It teaches us roles to play. It teaches us boy-girl games — special things to say and do. When I say I want to try for honesty, I mean the real things outside the meaningless patterns that we've been taught."

Her face as he watched had taken on an intensely serious and attentive expression. For the first time he was completely certain that there was no hint of a smile behind those large, round, green eyes. There was none at all, and he was very happy with this. And as he watched her he became aware of two things. They came to him with something of a shock. The first was that she was very nearly breastless. How had he missed that? And the other was that she was thin and long-limbed. Sitting there on the bed her birdlike figure had an odd spindly grace. It entered his mind that her bones were like neon tubes — unbelievably fragile and filled with thin white powder. For a moment he thought that they would shatter and collapse at the snap of a finger. She was nodding her head in agreement.

"Meaningless patterns . . ." she prompted, indicating that he should continue.

"But," he said, "can't you see that we have to do away with the accepted ideas of special sexual identities for men and women? We just have to do away with them."

"Okay," she agreed.

"And," he said, fighting for his words now, his head all of a sudden empty of everything but her sitting there attentively on the bed, ". . . and so . . . so what we've got to be, is . . . is you know, just us."

"Okay."

"And . . . help each other to find out." He discovered that for some time he'd been holding one arm in mid-gesture, frozen there by the realization of the naked and breastless and birdlike woman on his bed. He lowered the arm now, and as it was lowered one of Alberta's arms raised toward him and the other patted the space beside her on the bed. Alberta grinned at him.

II

"Well," she said, "was that just coupling?" There was no triumph in her eyes — only a look of confidence that praise would come.

"It was not!" Chevy said with as much conviction as he could muster. "It most definitely was not!" He would have said more since praise was deserved, but he did not quite know how to give that praise — how to fit words around it, so he just grinned and looked contented and hoped that that would do. But even if the grin satisfied her, it did not make him feel any more at ease. In his mind was a question concerning a green-eyed girl who had just taken off her clothes and jumped into his bed without waiting for him to finish seducing her, and as Chevy lay beside her he had not the slightest idea of why she had done it.

It had crossed his mind that she might have done it to shame him, or to challenge him and his ideas in some way. During those first few moments when nothing had yet been resolved it had crossed his mind that she might be at worst just a nymphomaniac, or at best simply an exhibitionist. Now, the resolution achieved and past, none seemed to be true.

She had passed up countless opportunities to shame him, to make him feel foolish. She could easily have unmanned him, sacrificing his ego to bolster her own, but she had not.

Why had she taken off her clothes? As he lay there Chevy's mind ground and clanged.

Once a girl had approached him and had coolly asked if he would please take her to bed. She had clinically selected him to help rid herself of her virginity. That one had said thank you and had left. There had been no question of motive there, but this one did not leave. She was not crying. She was not acting tough and hard, not shy and helpless, not offended and ravished or blasé. This one was grinning at him and waiting for praise, and though Chevy had been looking back at her with what he hoped was not total bafflement and mystification, now he was forced to lower his eyes, and since he knew neither how to give the praise that needed giving or how to ask the question that needed to be answered, he just started talking.

"Did you know," he said, "that I thought at first that you were a virgin? In the name of honesty, now, I really did." He did not smile when he said this, and he did not look at her.

"For a while there I thought you were, too," she said, and she smiled broadly, but he did not see it.

"It's true," he said seriously. "It's very difficult to tell about things like that. Not that it's important, of course.

But anyway, it's much better that you weren't. I was genuinely relieved."

"Much better for what?" she asked in a cautious voice.

"Much better for our relationship. The thing we talked about. The thing we agreed to try for. It would be much more difficult to attain if you had been a virgin. I was really relieved." He turned his face toward her with a serious look to show how relieved he was.

"You were relieved?" she said. "*Relieved?*"

"Sure."

"Really?"

"Absolutely."

"Man!" she said. In one quick scrambling movement she sat up on the bed and clasped her arms around her legs and peered at him narrowly. "I've never heard anybody say that before," she said. "Not after!"

"What? Say what?"

"That it's best *not* to be one. A virgin, I mean. Not *af*ter!"

"Really?" He looked up at her, lifting one of his eyebrows and speaking in a perfectly mild and unemphatic voice. "I wouldn't have one," he said.

"Wouldn't have a virgin?" She dropped her mouth open.

"You couldn't get me to marry one with a court order," he said. It was a topic he liked, and he felt he could express himself better on his feet. He left the bed and picked up two cigarettes and put them into one corner of his mouth while he organized his thoughts. On the bed Alberta was wearing an expression of attention much like the one she had worn at the movies when the stallion had walked casually under a ledge on which crouched a mountain lion.

"Normally," Chevy said, speaking in a purely conversational way, "I wouldn't have had anything to do with you if I'd thought you were a virgin."

"You knew I wasn't, huh? You could tell, huh?" Alberta was intrigued by his insight. She beamed at him and shook her head in amazement.

Chevy had not expected this question, and so he did not answer it. "Anybody with a maidenhead at your age," he said, "has got problems. Serious problems. I just wouldn't want to be acquainted with anybody that neurotic." He left her to consider this and began to search for matches. He had no sooner begun this than he forgot what he was looking for. He began methodically opening and closing the drawers of his dresser.

"No shit?" the girl on the bed said in a breathy excited voice. "Really?"

He turned his head toward her from the dresser. "What we're supposed to be feeling, of course, is guilt and shame." He laughed a murmuring laugh to himself at the very idea of such a concept. "But that's as out of date as virginity itself." He gave her this information dispassionately, leaving the dresser and advancing on the desk — again opening and closing drawers automatically. "Of course there are still young people who are limping along with the rules and the ideas of the old generation, but their numbers dwindle. We've all met them — prissy professional virgins. Those poor people who've been funnel-fed the old ideas of shame and guilt. The ones who don't even know what a personal relationship is. I'm really happy you aren't one of them."

"God, me too!" she burst out happily.

Chevy blinked once as if something had just been swung dangerously near his eyes. This had been his standard after-seduction speech, and when he had created it he had believed himself to have anticipated all possible reactions. This one had never occurred to him. He stared at her for just a moment, then turned and resumed his search for the matches — opening again the drawers of the dresser. There it was again — that impossible appearance of vulnerability, like an open and unattended Brinks truck. As Chevy opened the drawers he remembered the time when he had managed to take all the shell from an uncooked egg without puncturing the membrane. It was with that same shell-less look that she sat on his bed now. It was Tiny Tim and the cartoon bear — pervious and transparent and yet more durable and less fragile and at the same time more delicate than before. Chevy was unable, quite, to meet and hold her bright smiling eyes, but as he rose from the dresser and moved again to the desk he managed to sweep his gaze casually over her. She was grinning hugely, watching him, one hand hovering near her mouth as if prepared to stifle humor if it threatened to get out of control.

"What's so funny?" Chevy asked. He managed to smile himself.

She began to chuckle. "You were walking just like Genghis Khan."

"Who?"

"This rooster we used to have on the ranch named Genghis Khan." Alberta closed one eye, peering at him humorously out of the other, still chuckling.

"A rooster named *what?*" He had taken the cigarettes out of his mouth, and a smile tried to decide whether or not to settle there.

"This rooster we used to have would walk in a funny way," she said, "especially after he'd finished with some hen. He'd walk really fast with his neck-feathers all ruffled up and lifting his feet high, and . . ." She got off the bed and took a few steps to show him.

"Do I walk with my feet high?" Chevy looked at his feet.

"No, but your hair is all sticking up on end," she explained. "And you had the same look on your face as ol' Genghis used to." She waited for him to be amused by this, and so he laughed.

"A rooster named Genghis *Khan?*" he said. He had resumed his search for the matches, both cigarettes in his mouth again. "Who'd name a rooster Genghis Khan?"

"My father," Alberta said. "He had names for everything. He'd wait until he had just the right name. Most of the time it was, too. Just right for the thing."

"Jesus!" Chevy said. "Genghis Khan!" He was standing with the cigarettes by the hot-plate, waiting for it to warm, looking curiously at her.

"I was four before he named me." She looked at her knees in a way that told Chevy that she was remembering her father, and that it was not a wholly unpleasant memory.

"Really?" he said. "Alberta, huh? What's it mean?"

"For the Canadian province, I guess. I've never been there." She smiled warmly at her knee. "Sometimes he never did find the right name, and so he'd just call it 'that damn thing over there.' " She chuckled, remembering.

"What's your real name then?"

"Alberta is."

"Alberta? He waited until you were four to name you Alberta? What did he call you till then?"

"I don't remember," Alberta said. "But Alberta isn't bad. He named my brother Billy-the-Kid."

"*Named* him that?"

"Legal."

"Billy-the-*Kid*?"

"Billy-the-Kid Raynes. Most people think it's a kind of nickname, but it's his real name. They use it in the papers in quote marks, but they shouldn't." She stared now at her toes, wiggling them, then after a moment added: "He's kind of famous."

The hot-plate was glowing, but Chevy just stood there looking at her. "How?" he said after a minute. It occurred to him absurdly that the brother was a bandit, and he pictured him with a handkerchief across the lower half of his face, each hand holding a long pistol. The eyes above the bandana were Alberta's eyes.

"Rodeo," Alberta said. "Bareback bronc, mostly, but he rides Brahmas a lot too." She continued to examine her toes, and Chevy saw that they were long and delicately formed and unexpectedly sensual. "That is when he isn't all crippled up with a broken leg. He's little," she explained with a wave of her hand, still not looking at him, ". . . little like me, and he's got thin bones kind of and most of the time he's got a broken leg. He had a lot of his pants made with a special zipper along the sides of the leg so that they'll expand to fit the cast when one of his legs are broke." She wiggled the toes slowly, one at a time, watching them intently, as if something important were at stake in their movement. Then, in a lower register: "I read about the zippers in a magazine article."

Chevy suddenly became aware of the heat of the burner, and he lit the two cigarettes, squinting against the glow, then came to the bed and handed her one.

"I don't smoke," she said, "but I don't mind." She took the cigarette, holding it like a straw connecting a girl in a calendar to a strawberry soda, but she did not put it in her mouth.

"Rodeo rider?" Chevy asked.

She nodded. "You have any brothers or sisters?"

"No," Chevy said. "I don't."

She continued to look only at the toes, smiling a secret kind of smile. "In the article he said that I was the only member of the family still living, and that I was lost."

After a moment he asked, "Is it true? What he said?"

"Naw. That's just kind of a secret message. He knew I'd see it. I haven't seen him in about five years. Nobody has. I mean in our family." She was still looking at her toes, moving them now one by one as if playing some exotic and invisible musical instrument. When Chevy did not comment she continued. "He looks more like a dancer or something than a bareback rider."

For a moment they both watched her toes, then Chevy looked at his cigarette, amazed to see by the long, curving ash that he had not yet put it to his lips. He cupped his hand under it and went in search of an ashtray. He found one and carried it to the fat-armed chair. "Where did you say you were from?" he said. This suddenly seemed to him to be a very critical bit of information.

Alberta looked up suspiciously.

"No! I mean really! I really want to know." He lifted his eyebrows.

She told him the name of the state and then of the town. "The saddest, dumpiest, crummiest town you have ever . . ." She tipped her head and narrowed her eyes. "Boy, the first time I get me a plane and some bombs . . ." She spread her arms and reviewed the mission she would fly on her home town, then looked up to see if he was smiling, and he was. "Shit," she said. "I sure feel good." She awkwardly took a mouthful of smoke and blew it toward the ceiling. "Actually, though, I've got two homes. There was the home where I lived in the mountains until I was fourteen and a half. It was more like a hide-out than a home, you know? Like in westerns where the bad guys hole up after they've robbed the stage. Then we moved to the crummy town. At the mountain town I almost had a horse. I was going to get one just when we left."

Chevy could see that this fact still held excitement for her.

"Hey!" she said, bouncing to her knees on the bed. "Neat! We're actually talking. I'm actually talking. How about that?"

"How about that?" Chevy echoed because he could think of nothing else to say. But he smiled a very encouraging smile.

"Thanks," she said, and he could tell she really meant it. "I'm the poor bastard who's always listening to everybody's problems. I never get to talk at all. If I was laying in the hospital dying of double cancer and in an oxygen tent all the doctors would want to come in and tell me their problems. I *know* they would. You'd never believe the amount of problems I've listened to," she said. "It'd numb you. Really!"

"Sympathetic face?" Chevy suggested stupidly. He remembered to take a drag from his cigarette.

"Maybe," she said, and she reached up and touched her cheekbones briefly. "No," she decided. "It's just that I'm dumb enough to listen." She started to smile, and then the smile collapsed into a look of sorrow. "Like the kids I'd run around with in high school," she said in a softer voice than she'd been using. "They'd tell me all their problems, and I'd sympathize, I really would, and they'd tell me really personal things and swear me to secrecy and then the next day they'd be spreading the word that they spent the night in the back seat screwing me or something." She twisted her mouth into a wry smile.

"Goddamn people!" Chevy said, incensed and getting suddenly to his feet. "It's guilt and shame that does it! Guilt and shame. What we've got to do is to . . ."

"Right," said Alberta, ". . . the bastards. That's why I wanted to be a private detective." Her fingers had been tracing the pattern on the bedspread, but now she looked up. "Of course that was when I was a kid." It was meant to be an explanation.

"Private detective?" Chevy asked, clearing his throat and sitting down as inconspicuously as possible.

"Didn't I tell you about that yet? No, I guess not." A shy grin passed over her face, and she quickly wrinkled up her nose to hide the shy part of it. "But anyway I sent for this course out of one of Dad's magazines. I had to lie about my age and say my name was Albert instead of Alberta, but I passed about a million lessons. I did everything but send away for the final examination and get the license and all that. But for that I'd have had to go before some state board, and I was only sixteen. It cost me a bunch of money. I still have some finger-print powder around somewhere."

Chevy remembered again about his cigarette. He brought it hopefully to his lips, but it had gone out.

"But it was really neat. When all the girls in high school were going around calling me a punchboard, all I was doing was going around listening to people's problems and offering to solve all their crimes." She chuckled to herself at this. ". . . and most of those girls who were talking about me were running around so full of penicillin they sloshed whenever . . ."

"Clap? Gonorrhea?" Chevy managed to say. There was an involuntary tightening in his loins.

"Yeah, and I didn't go down once from the time I was fourteen and a half until I was seventeen. Not since I got to the new town. Not once. But some guy from the mountain town . . . remember? Where I almost had a horse? Anyway he came through and spread the word. Some creep. Byron Clausberg was his stupid name. I remember him. He had breath like some old bandage."

Chevy put one hand in his hair and raked it through slowly. "How about before you were fourteen and a half?" he said with a little laugh. It was meant to sound jolly.

She looked up, uncertain. "Do you mind? I'm not embarrassing you or anything, am I?"

"No! Embarrassing? Hell no! Talk! Fine!" Chevy said. "People keep things like this hidden inside of them too much. I mean why shouldn't we talk about our first experiences since . . ." He made a limp gesture and cleared his throat again.

"Well," she said, shy again and wrinkling up her nose. "The first time was when I was ten, and my brother . . ."

"Your *brother!*" He couldn't help it.

"Well, he was only fourteen . . ."

"No! I didn't *mean* anything. Just that it's interesting since there seems to be a lot of incest among pre . . . aah . . . pre-pubescents. Statistically," he added absurdly.

"Well, anyway, he said he'd give me this toy he had. I don't remember even what it was. Even then though the news got around pretty fast, and pretty soon we had most of the toys in town." She chuckled, looking up to see if he had appreciated this.

"Heh, heh," Chevy said.

"Until I was fourteen and a half I didn't even know it was dangerous or anything." She bunched her lips and tilted her head, looking relieved.

Chevy cleared his throat again. "Clap?" he inquired

casually. "Where did you go to school? I mean what kind of a high school . . ." He finished with an empty flap of the hand.

"Well, it wasn't exactly clap. It was just the sores that they got from the plastic wrap. But for a while . . ."

"Plastic wrap?" Chevy asked, floundered.

"Like you put around pieces of tomato and onion and things and put them in the refrigerator to keep them from spoiling, you know? Well, the boys were wrapping a foot or so of plastic wrap around it and away they go." She wrapped a finger and held it up, chuckling.

"Plastic wrap?"

"Well, there was a guy selling rubbers at a service station, but the League for Decency or somebody came along and closed him up so everybody started to use this wrap."

"Wrap?" The crease had appeared between Chevy's eyes. "And it gave people the *clap?*" Chevy was not laughing at all.

"It gave girls sores, see . . ." Alberta left the bed with her cigarette and put it out at the sink. ". . . and there was a really big deal about it, but the thing was that I wasn't doing anything, and they were all talking about me." She chuckled again. "All I was doing was going around solving crimes."

After a moment Chevy said, "But you didn't go down once after you were fourteen and a half." His face remained impassive.

"Right."

"And not again till you were seventeen."

"Not once," she said happily.

They were grinning at each other across the room, and Chevy knew that this was the moment to ask her why she had taken off her clothes as she had, and in the manner and at the time that she had, but Alberta started to speak first.

"You weren't lying, were you, about the virgins," she said. "You weren't lying about anything, were you. You're really interested in the stuff I was telling you about me. I could tell." She had continued to smile, pleased, and although he knew that he should not, Chevy looked away at the full ashtray in his hand.

"By God," she said, "you're about the best guy I ever met. After all the times I was wrong about guys, you know, it was worth it to be right this one time."

And Chevy, flattered, blushing and suddenly shy, sitting across from her naked in his chair, still holding the dead and cold cigarette, had nothing to say. He was wondering if maybe she hadn't been right. Maybe he'd been a virgin after all.

INDE-
PENDENCE
DAY

NOISELESS PATIENT SPIDER

A noiseless patient spider,
I mark'd where on a little promontory it stood
isolated,
Mark'd how to explore the vacant vast surrounding,
It launch'd forth filament, filament, filament, out
of itself,
Ever unreeling them, ever tirelessly speeding them.

Walt Whitman

The house Daniel and Ellen found was at 648 Vassar Street, in the newest section of the city, just a few blocks from Mrs. Blake's own house. It was far too nice, and of course far too expensive, but Mrs. Blake had insisted that they at least look at it.

It had everything they wanted or needed with the unexpected addition of a kitchen so modern and perfect that it made Ellen's mouth begin to quiver when she saw it. Daniel had noticed and he walked over and put his arm around her shoulders and said: "You like it, honey?" and Ellen had not been able to say a word, just nod her head. The kitchen had built-in cupboards of an unknown but deep-textured and expensive-looking wood, and they had handles and knobs of weathered copper, and part of one wall was real brick with an oven built into it, and the ceiling was beamed with sturdy rough beams. The oven, stove and refrigerator were of a matching rich-hued brown-orange — the color of strong tea — and they were lit brilliantly by the large window which opened over the stainless sink and out into the yard. Ellen went and stood there by the window and looked out, and Daniel noticed that she let her hands rest in the bottom of the sink as if she had been interrupted in the middle of dishwashing by something pleasant happening outside. This made Daniel think that she hadn't noticed the brown-orange dishwasher, and he was ready to point this out to her when she turned from the window and looked first at Daniel and then at his mother with a fierce look of gratitude and joy which took Daniel's words away and left all three of them quiet and reverent for several minutes.

Daniel had made up his mind to yield in many things, and he would have yielded instantly to her desires about the house even if he had not liked it himself, but as it turned out, Daniel liked the house very much. The only feature with which he might have found fault was the bedroom in the basement. It had already been completed by the former occupant. In inspecting it, however, Daniel saw that the job had been very inexpertly done in the first place, and there would definitely be some work to do down there — some remodeling and some rebuilding. There was space in the basement for a large recreation room, and standing there alone, his mother and wife-to-be still in the kitchen, Daniel began to dream that this would be his domain. He saw that he could partition off a room, a den. There would be space for a pool table which he would buy and recondition. He could build a bar in the corner with a portion that lifted up to allow him to slip behind. At the other end would be bookshelves and an old sofa and chair where he could sit and read. It would be a warm room, well-lit. A place where a man could go with other men to play poker or have a drink, or where he could just go and sit alone.

Two days later, after they had taken the house, his mother surprised Ellen with a matching washer and dryer, and there was no way to avoid putting them in the basement. Ellen began to talk about having him build a washroom down there, pointing out that there was a drain built into the floor which showed where the washroom was supposed to be. The drain, Daniel saw, was right exactly under the place where the pool table was to have been.

He did not let on. The house was to be Ellen's to decide on. The house that he had provided for her was far better than anything she or her family had ever had or ever hoped to have, and Daniel wanted her joy in it to be unmodified by anything. He agreed that of course she would have the washroom.

They had found and taken the house just three weeks before the wedding day, and nearly every day for those three weeks they had come there to clean a little or to install some small item they had bought or to rearrange the furniture that Mrs. Blake had surprised them with. They had debated for two whole days and decided finally to open a charge account at an exclusive furniture store, and under this account they had picked out curtains, a new rug for the living room, and a queen-sized bed. They also bought other items of furniture and had a terrible fight over a lamp which Ellen had decided she wanted — an expensive, tall, very heavy affair of welded metal which Daniel insisted was against the grain of everything else in the front room — totally out of place. But Ellen had gotten it, and after a few days Daniel admitted that he didn't mind it so much after all.

With the house there had somehow been no time to think about or talk about the baby. For a while Daniel had given private thought to finding a name for it, but when he mentioned this to Ellen she had given him a surprised and hurt look which told him he was out of order by talking about the baby at this time, and so he put off thinking about it. Seven months would be a long time. It would be winter then, and now it was only spring. There was a long time before they would have to think seriously about it. It was progressing without help from either of them.

They waited. Although the stove was in the kitchen, Daniel could not persuade Ellen to make so much as a snack or a pot of coffee on it. She would not cook in the kitchen until they were moved in and until she could have all the equipment — much of it still to be furnished, they expected, by wedding gifts — and it was the same situation with the queen-sized bed. At first Daniel had tried to dissuade her with the logic of the situation, but at heart he was in sympathy and was glad.

Although Daniel had previously planned to leave Easton to work a few years in a larger city, now it was clear that he should begin immediately to learn his mother's business, and he became formally employed at Blake Realty at a good but not extravagant salary.

Although they knew it would be very difficult, they

agreed not to talk about the house or to show it to anyone. The day after the wedding, they would leave on their honeymoon, but the evening of the wedding day, after the reception which would be held at Mrs. Blake's home, they would have a party for their friends — a small, private get-together for ten or twelve. It would be a gesture against the tradition of the blushing bride and the eager groom. It would be a good way to start this marriage of theirs which was not to be an ordinary marriage.

As the three weeks passed and as the plans for the party and the wedding began to expand, the two events — party and wedding — began to loom with nearly equal importance. Ellen, although she had never actually been ashamed of her father's house, had never been able to bring her friends to it. With brothers and sisters it had been a crowded and a far too public place. Daniel too had somehow never managed to host a real party.

So the party grew in proportion, threatening to overpower and dwarf the wedding ceremony itself. With his first paycheck from his mother's real estate office, Daniel laid in quite a large stock of liquor, and Ellen, with growing anxiety, read books on etiquette, writing lists of ingredients for exotic hors d'oeuvres and notes of encouragement and advice to herself in a cramped, tiny, paralyzed scrawl. These she taped everywhere in the house, on mirrors and cupboards and doors.

When they talked about it they found themselves quarreling, and at the end of the quarrel they would walk silently and stiffly through the house, avoiding each other's eyes. Then, passing each other in a doorway, they would fall into each other's arms and Ellen would cry and they would tell each other that it was all right — that everything was all right — and they would begin to smile, thinking of themselves as they would be after the party — their arms around each other's waists bidding warm goodbyes at the door to their friends, then turning to each other in warmth and luxury and perhaps mixing one more drink for themselves while they talked over the evening's events, and then retiring to the queen-sized bed.

It especially pleased Daniel to think of things this way. It proved to him that it was the companionship and the love and the oneness which was important and not just the sex. The party proved that it was the whole house that mattered, not just the bedroom.

II

From her earliest high school days Ellen had dreamed with perfect confidence and certainty of the person she would someday become. Her heroine and her idol was not a living figure, not a movie star or a fashion model; it was her own future self. It was the perfect and perfected Ellen of the future who stood so clearly in her mind and who was the guiding figure of her life.

Ellen had been acutely conscious from early youth that what she did then — what she learned and how she allowed herself to be molded — would have immeasurable effect in later years, and she carefully attended to her development, feeling awed by the knowledge that she, the awkward, shy child, should have such influence, such intimate concert with the finished adult. When Ellen picked up a pen to write a book report, she did so with a reverence, aware that the very slant of the handwriting was in the process of crystallization.

Ellen saw what the world honored in women and what it despised. Watching her two older sisters mature and lose favor, Ellen began to realize how the future Ellen would be created. She would do nothing that was wrong, as the sisters had done. She would learn from them what not to do. She would do nothing that might soil or tarnish her sensibilities or cast a questionable light upon the purity of her intentions.

This was the dream that moved Ellen to work and study and sacrifice and miss out, and there was never a doubt that it was a good and a plausible dream. In her last years of high school she was aware that dozens of mothers were saying to their daughters, "Why can't you be more like Ellen Curry?"

Ellen was a good girl.

But by the beginning of her second year at the university, belief in the dream was all gone. It had not been snatched cruelly from her, but had disappeared like a spring snowbank — imperceptibly until it was difficult to remember that it had ever been there. At nineteen Ellen looked around and began to realize with something like despair that the girls who had not been conscious of the responsibility of creating themselves, who had been not only uncaring or unknowing but absolutely flagrant with defying the unquestionable rules of such a creation — these girls had become somehow far, far closer to the ideal than she had. They were more cultured, sophisticated, knowing. They had something which Ellen did not know — a secret, mysterious knowledge. She could see it in their eyes — their amused, knowing eyes.

Since she had not become what she had dreamed, Ellen was forced to examine the thing that she had become instead, and this examination hurled her from mere disappointment and dismay and vague unhappiness to utter despair.

Ellen began to feel like nothing at all.

In the beginning of that second year Ellen began to wear dark glasses from morning till night, and she began not to care properly for her hair or her face or her nails. While she had always had at least a pleasant — her mother's friends said "sweet" — personality, she began to be sullen and moody and preoccupied.

But some things changed. She stopped working for the college newspaper, the *Eastoner*, where she had been a general helper with no real title. She had just quit although she felt that she stood a good chance of perhaps being even an editor in another year. Why be an editor? Why? Why be anything? From pure force of habit she had tried through it all to maintain her grades and her studies. But she was tired all the time, falling asleep behind her books and in class and even at work — once having been awakened by Mr. Ross himself.

Finally Ellen went to the campus medical center to see if perhaps she might have mononucleosis. At the center they had given her a test for the mono, but they had also insisted that she submit to a pregnancy test. Ellen, bewildered, shocked, and at the same time challenged, consented. Both tests were negative, but they left Ellen feeling stunned. Pregnancy? She began to look around her and to study the other girls in her classes. Pregnancy?

Ellen was by no means a stupid girl, and she had never considered herself naïve, and yet it dawned on her that perhaps the values which she had assigned to things, the value judgments so inflexibly and thoughtlessly accepted, perhaps these were wrong. She had always assumed that she was alone because she was so far ahead on this narrow path to perfection. She began now to understand that she was the only one on the path.

Pregnancy? Ellen began to understand where the other path was. She began to think she knew what the secret was.

Ellen's life changed directions sharply. She failed a French test. Her grades slid, and only shortly after her test at the health center Ellen got rid of her virginity.

She had gone to sit at the Student Union Building the night before the French exam, determined to fail it, and a boy with the beginnings of a beard appeared at her table and without asking, sat. Within fifteen minutes they were walking toward his apartment, and when they arrived there, again without asking, he made love to her four times. After the fourth and final time he had fallen asleep, and Ellen collected her clothing and left, feeling secret and very smug. Now she had turned the tables. Now she knew something that the world didn't know.

Although she abandoned her sunglasses, people who knew Ellen were shocked and alarmed to see her violating all of their expectations. But Ellen was a happier person. She would burst out laughing or would begin, at strange and unpredictable times, to smile secretly to herself. Today, tomorrow, tonight — *any*thing was possible. The diet was over. She was off the wagon. She would miss out no more.

One of the first things she did was to seek out and secure the friendship of Chrystal Morrisey, a girl who seemed to have found a way of living which brought her respect and admiration from many quarters. Chrystal would have been considered slightly wild by the old Ellen, and the new Ellen's parents began to worry, nervously beginning long talks every few days until Ellen silenced them by suggesting that she might leave home for an apartment of her own — perhaps with Chrystal Morrisey.

Chrystal had a great deal she could teach Ellen. She had a way of standing and talking which left no doubt that Chrystal Morrisey knew what was happening. She had acquired a way of dropping her lower jaw and sucking in her cheeks to produce a regal, sunken look which Ellen much admired, and she spoke in an urgent whisper and said things in a pointed manner which made her words deeply and profoundly felt.

But Ellen was an apt student, and in direct competition with Chrystal, and after only a few months' study, she won Daniel.

She met him after a meeting of the Students for a Democratic Society — a campus organization formed and led by Daniel's friend Chevy Callister. It was a not-quite-sanctioned group of beards and bright eyes and, reputedly, the school's intellectual element. Ellen had begun to attend some of the meetings with Chrystal Morrisey, and no one had made them feel unwelcome. After the second meeting she and Chrystal found themselves talking to Daniel. Ellen found him not unattractive. He was excessively wiry and tense-seeming and listened attentively to the comments which she made about the meeting. From the first he seemed more interested in Ellen than in Chrystal, and when Chrystal realized this she rose to the competition confidently and with the air of one giving a lesson. But Ellen swept Daniel from under the amazed eyes of Chrystal Morrisey and drove with him to the rimrocks and there, with the lights of the city spread under them, they talked and made love until, very late, Daniel fell asleep.

It had not been Ellen's intention to settle down with one man, but her victory over Chrystal had inflated Daniel's worth so tremendously that when he continued to call her up, she continued to go with him. She got a prescription for The Pill, but she could never seem to remember to take them. And so, in the fourth month after meeting Daniel, she found herself pregnant.

For two terrible days after the pregnancy was confirmed her life plunged again, and she considered suicide as the only solution. She considered it seriously enough to sit with her forehead leaning on the top of her father's loaded pump bird-gun for nearly an hour. What dissuaded her from this approach finally was the fear that since she could not easily reach the trigger she might succeed only in injuring and disfiguring herself. Her next idea was to buy sleeping pills, and again, she was serious enough to take money to the drugstore, only to find that she must have a prescription for the really powerful ones.

When she allowed herself to be taken to meet Daniel's mother, she had not yet given up the idea of self-destruction, but had only put off the act itself in the search for the perfect means.

But from the day that she met Mrs. Blake, Ellen's life again changed direction radically. The forgotten dream caught up with her again and became, unbelievably, a reality. The pregnancy which she hated and feared and abhorred was viewed with reverence and joy, and the eyes and hands of Daniel's mother promised love forever, and comfort forever, and dignity forever and forever.

III

So Ellen was married in a large, white wedding, and she was standing by the door of her new house and the guests were coming in — her first guests. Her husband, her Daniel, was mixing drinks for people in the kitchen — she could hear him and the clinking of the ice and the laughter.

She walked to a place where she could see him through the kitchen door. He had changed from the tuxedo and into a suit although she had asked him not to. He had looked so nice in it — so dashing. She watched his nervous, quick gestures — measuring, mixing — and a warmness washed over her. There was a quality about him and about his mother and about some of his mother's friends who had been at the wedding — a charm, a graciousness.

You noticed this quality even before you heard them speak, and when they spoke there was no doubt about it at all. Her Daniel had it, this charm, and it was what she wanted. It was what she would have — the poise, the ease which they had.

But her Daniel was not *too* charming. He was not soft and foppish, not her Daniel with his hard, wiry body and with his incredible earnestness which got him into so much trouble and which made him so sweet and so human. Sweet, dashing Daniel with his fumbling earnestness and his toppled poise. He was her husband, her man. And although there was much that Ellen expected to learn from his mother and from him, it was a comfort to know that he too had things to learn. Some of them, perhaps, even from her.

And today she had finally left the one world and had entered this other, this new and infinitely possible world which tomorrow would place her — where? Tomorrow would be her honeymoon, and the bags sat, packed beside the queen-sized bed, and in them were hidden the plane tickets.

Where were the tickets for? How would she feel in Harold's in Reno, or in a taxi on Sunset Strip, or on The Loop in Chicago, or in San Francisco or New York? Where *was* he taking her? Why must it be such a secret? But any of those places would be perfect, any of them or a dozen others would be more than she could expect.

Daniel realized that he was being watched and left the group he was talking to and came out of the kitchen toward her. He put his arms around her and led her off to a place alone and he kissed her beside one ear. His breath, she noticed, was already quite heavy with whiskey. To Ellen whiskey had always seemed more directly related to drunkenness than other liquors. It seemed low, somehow, and common, and she wondered why he drank it. Why not scotch or vodka?

"Don't drink too much, Daniel," she reminded him with a smile.

"How do you think it's going?" he asked anxiously.

"It hasn't started yet," she told him. "Where's Chrystal, do you think?" Chrystal had been Ellen's maid of honor.

"Why?"

"Well, normally she's early for everything."

"The other day you told me she was always late for everything," he said.

Ellen didn't reply to this, but looked intently around the room as if another search might discover her missing friend.

"Maybe it's the rain," she said. The rain had begun — almost pointedly, Ellen thought — just as they had left the church.

"No rain in here," Daniel said, and he held his hands out, making a funny face.

Ellen put one of her arms around him. "Not in *our* house," she said.

"God!" Daniel said. He took a deep breath and rocked up on his toes, sweeping the room with his eyes. "This is ours, sweetheart," he said.

"And you're mine," she said, and she looked at him with a loving look.

"And you're *mine,*" he said. The two warm loving looks met for an instant, then fled. "God!" Daniel said again expansively.

"Daniel," she said, and she reached out and took his hand. "Aren't you going to give me even the littlest, teensiest . . ."

"Nope," he said. "Surprise. How can it be a surprise if . . ."

"But Daniel, it's tomorrow *mor*ning. Just a hint . . ."

"Well," he said, and he looked secretive and sly, raising one eyebrow. He wagged a cautioning finger at her. "You'll be seeing some very majestic and tall and magnificent things." He backed away from her toward the kitchen, smiling and wagging his finger.

"That's no hint," she called after him.

But of course it was. It was to be New York, of course. NEW YORK! Manhattan! Greenwich Village! Washington Square! Staten Island Ferry! NEW YORK! It was a place where women were tall and thin and did things with a carefully measured and gray-eyed grace. Men wore hats there and carried umbrellas. She and Daniel entered the picture. She saw herself on the Ferry. Behind her rose the rainbow of Wall Street buildings, but Ellen was uninterested by this. Her hair blew free and long and she gazed languidly . . .

The door buzzer sounded.

Ellen shook herself free of her dream and hurried to the door, feeling as if she had great news to tell whoever might be there. It was Chrystal.

"Ellen," Chrystal said, going into her arms briefly. "What a lovely, exquisite home. I didn't know . . ."

"Do you like it?" Ellen asked. She was suddenly without words, suddenly shy.

"I *love* it, ohhhh! It's all so lovely . . ." Chrystal seemed overcome and leaned into Ellen's arms again for a moment, then, clasping her by the shoulders, she leaned back and the two women studied each other with sad, tilted faces. "I'm so happy for you, Ellen," Chrystal said, and she allowed herself to be led down the hall to the bedroom where her raincoat was deposited, while she was permitted to examine the room.

"Lovely!" she exclaimed. "Just lovely."

At the kitchen Ellen's joy began to skitter out of control, and although she was aware that she was talking too much and too fast, she was not able to control it. "I wish it was light enough so that you could see the backyard," Ellen was saying. "So big. You can watch out into it from the kitchen window there. So big! And you can see everything that happens out there. As if anything ever happens in a backyard, ha ha."

Chrystal looked obligingly out the darkened window. "Lovely," she murmured.

"Fix Chrystal a drink, Daniel," Ellen said. "What is it? Brandy? No. *I'm* drinking brandy. What *is* it that you drink, Chrystal? Oh . . . something with scotch in it. Scotch and soda." She giggled merrily. "We'll be in the living room, Daniel."

In the living room, with abandon, Ellen confessed.

"We're jetting to New York for our honeymoon," she said.

"Oh, Ellen, you're so lucky. Be sure to see the Metropolitan Museum and the Guggenheim when you're there.

They're close. You can walk from one to the other, you know, and . . ."

"Yes," Ellen said. "I know." She sipped from her brandy. "Don't say a word to Daniel. It's supposed to be a secret."

"You're so lucky," Chrystal said.

"Yes, I know."

One of the bridesmaids, a friend of both Ellen and Chrystal, appeared at Ellen's other elbow. When she had first entered the house she had been interested only in displaying her date, a darkly handsome South American student whose English was not too good, and she had not yet commented on the house.

"How did you ever find this place?" she now asked. "Was it one of Mrs. Blake's?"

"We found it *through* her, yes," Ellen said, still not having forgiven the girl's original lack of enthusiasm. "She's in real estate, you know."

"Isn't it lovely?" Chrystal asked everyone. Everyone agreed that it was and Ellen was prepared to mention some especially attractive points, but the bridesmaid spoke again.

"Where did you find that unique *lamp*, Ellen?" she said, nodding toward the iron floor model. The tone was blandly inquisitive, but Ellen saw through it immediately.

"I don't know what I'm going to do with it," Ellen said.

"Oh?" Chrystal said warily.

"It must have cost Mrs. Blake a fortune," Ellen said. "It was one of her gifts, you know. But the lines are completely wrong for this room, don't you think?"

"It's a beautiful piece of furniture," Chrystal said, with

a breathtaking display of diplomacy, "but it doesn't really belong to this room, does it?"

"No," the bridesmaid assented. "It certainly doesn't."

"I'm going to have to send it back after the honeymoon," Ellen said. "Mrs. Blake is a dear, but this is, after all, *my* house."

Ellen was unable to tell how this was received. The doorbell rang and allowed her to make what seemed to be a perfectly-timed exit.

But this time when she approached the door she felt saddened. It was not going well — not as she had planned. There was no joy in it, no real beauty as it had always seemed there would be. It had been slowly dawning on her that she had somehow pictured the party not as action, not as a continuum of life and vitality, but rather as a series of stills in which she welcomed, showed, served and bade good-bye. She had not ever really considered that there were other things which must fill the time between, and now a hitherto hidden door swung open in Ellen's mind revealing a roomful of unconsidered possibilities. Guests must be introduced, conversations started and maintained. She had known that this must be done — certainly she had known. How had she forgotten? She and she alone was responsible for the life and the vitality that so far did not seem to be in her party, and she would be responsible for what would happen. Ellen's stomach tightened and her mind began to grow white around the edges as she realized this, and it was not with joy and gladness that she opened her front door to find Chevy Callister and a slight, pretty girl she had not seen before.

"I'm certain I have the wrong house," Chevy said loudly, not coming in. "The address checks out, but I know my buddy Daniel doesn't live in a crassly materialistic, bourgeoisie house like this."

"Yes, he does!" Daniel burst from the kitchen. "Come in, come in. Who's this . . . Alberta? Where have you been hiding this girl? C'mon in. Have a drink."

Daniel led them immediately into the kitchen without giving Ellen a chance to take their coats. Ellen was glad, however, to have been spared the necessity of talking to Chevy. Everything he said seemed to have two meanings. He always seemed to be mocking her. She never knew quite when to laugh. And who was that girl? She had walked with the two men toward the kitchen, having not so much as glanced casually toward the rug. The word "chippy" entered Ellen's mind and was accepted without reservation or question. Ellen viewed the subconscious as a vast storehouse of absolute knowledge which was not to be questioned when it accidentally yielded up such information. Had she continued in college, she might have majored in psychology, and to Ellen the word was a revelation. She watched the girl, her coat still on, disappearing into the kitchen. The raincoat, she saw, was one of those things that they make too many of somewhere which hang rack after rack in cut-rate clothing stores like uniforms.

"Chippy," thought Ellen. Then Daniel appeared from the kitchen carrying the two coats, Chevy's and the chippy's, and he took them to the bedroom. Then he came to her and kissed her lightly on the cheek.

"Chevy and I are going to go down to the basement for

a minute, okay? I want to show him what I'm going to do down there." He kissed her again. "Hold down the fort, okay?"

A moment later he disappeared into the basement with Chevy, and Ellen took a deep breath and moved toward the now deserted kitchen to busy herself with making the hors d'oeuvres available. They were on trays under towels, ready to be served. She removed the towel from one and saw in a heart-stopping, chilly moment beyond agony that something had happened to her special herring-paste sandwiches. They were soggy. The moisture had seeped into the bread turning it a weak-looking green.

And there was no garbage can! Why hadn't they bought a garbage can? They should have known no one would provide that at the wedding or the shower! In despair Ellen opened a drawer beside the sink and scooped the sandwiches into it. She filled the hole they left on the tray with potato chips and ventured bravely with it into the living room. She wondered suddenly how hors d'oeuvres were served. Was there a special place they should be put, or should she continue to hold them? More and more things were coming up that she had forgotten to prepare herself for. She placed the tray on the coffee table, and left the area quickly. She noticed the girl Chevy had brought standing alone and running her fingers over the iron lamp in a nervous unsure way, and she moved immediately toward her, overcome by goodwill and magnanimity and thankful for having something positive to do.

"Don't you have a drink yet?" Ellen asked her, swirling her own refilled brandy glass.

"I'm not much of a drinker," the girl offered. She seemed grateful for the attention, and she smiled a shy and rather awkward smile.

"Perhaps scotch and soda?"

"That's okay." Ellen began to walk toward the kitchen and the girl followed her. "It's not that I don't want to drink. I mean I don't think it's wrong," the girl said. "But every time I drink I start to say all kinds of profound things and at the same time I get the hiccups. And who'll pay attention to profound things if the guy who's saying them has the hiccups, you know? So why bother, do you see? They cancel each other out, so I might as well not drink." They were in the kitchen now and Ellen saw the girl press her lips together unhappily as if she wished she could call the words back and start over.

"Really?" Ellen laughed softly. She was feeling much better.

"So I don't drink much," the girl said. "But I don't mind. By the way, I'm Alberta Raynes." She held her hand out like a man, curled and prepared to grab, and Ellen took it gingerly for a moment by the fingers, wondering if perhaps it should have been her duty as hostess to make the self-introduction. She couldn't remember reading anything about that, but she had no sooner considered it than she realized that she was responsible for mixing the drink for the girl, and she had no idea how to do it.

"Do you mind waiting for Daniel to mix your drink?" she asked coolly. "Scotch and soda is his specialty, and he'd just be upset if I didn't allow him to make it." She thought about that for a moment. "Well, not up*set*, but you know how husbands are." She gave another small laugh, and the girl returned a startlingly broad smile, the lips up-pointed and tight together. It seemed the smile of someone who is not at ease or comfortable, and Ellen was overcome with compassion. She began to feel amiable and protective and more secure in the role of hostess, and she decided to try to cheer the girl.

"We're going to New York for our honeymoon," she said.

"Hey," said the girl. "Neat!" She seemed genuinely happy about it.

"We're jetting there tomorrow morning. Have you ever been there?"

"I'd never even been to Easton till a few months ago."

Ellen couldn't help smiling, but not at the girl.

"I can hardly wait to get to the Metropolitan Museum again," Ellen said over the edge of her glass. "That's within walking distance of the Guggenheim, you know."

"What's a Guggenheim?"

Ellen lowered her jaw a little and let her cheeks sink in. "It's a museum," she said. She made a square with her hands. "For pictures . . . ?"

"That the one that goes around?" The girl made a vague spiral with one hand. "By that guy Wright?"

Ellen gave her a pitying but amiable look. "No," she said. "That one's in Chicago."

"Oh," the girl said. "That's news," and she looked away from Ellen and around the room again, reaching out curiously to place her fingers on the brick wall. Ellen felt immediately guilty about her deception, but since this girl doubtless didn't know anyway, and since it as well might be in Chicago as anyplace else — and since she was going out of her way to talk to this girl in the first place, she didn't see any reason why she should worry about offending her. Ellen began to feel a distant dislike for the girl building, but she felt obliged to stay with her until Daniel returned.

"How long have you known Chevy?" Ellen asked.

"About a month," the girl said.

"Have you met his father?" Ellen had always been uncertain of exactly how to take the fact of Chevy's father. To her it had always been the single most mystifying fact about him.

"I met him formally," the girl said. "He booted me out of school once."

"Oh!" Ellen said with a little gasp. "I remember now. Weren't there articles in the paper and everything?" And then she didn't know what to say next, so she took a small drink of her brandy. Ellen remembered clearly why the girl had been refused admission, and she also remembered that the girl had been something of a heroine with the Students for a Democratic Society crowd. "You were something of a *cause célèbre*, weren't you?" she asked. She gave the real French pronunciation to the words. "Believe me, I'm completely in accord with your problem."

"It's not my problem," the girl said.

Perhaps Ellen didn't hear. She was thinking with some pride that she had found a topic of conversation about which they could both talk with interest. One by one she was overcoming each problem she was faced with as a hostess. "This whole problem of *in loco parentis* is a most central one for our generation, don't you think?"

"Most," said the girl, nodding.

"Our generation is a generation of revolution," Ellen said, beginning to speak in an intense low whisper, "and we will make a world where each of us has the right and privilege to judge our own actions for ourselves."

The girl had nothing to add to the fullness of this.

"For example," Ellen continued, "most people might consider this little party . . ." she waved a hand ". . . to be shockingly unorthodox, but Daniel and I feel that as educated people it's incumbent upon us to be a conscious part of this revolution. We want a marriage based on equality and freedom and intelligence."

"Good for you," the girl said.

"I'm not, after all," Ellen said, sucking in her cheeks, "a blushing bride in the old sense." She meant, of course, that she was a modern girl, a girl of her generation, but this was somehow missed.

"That's great," the girl said. "Just come right out and be honest about it. This frilly crap makes me nauseous anyway. Oh," she mewed, mincing, "look at the pretty virrr-gin."

Ellen was stunned. She realized instantly that she had been betrayed and despair rose in her like a balloon. Daniel must have told Chevy about the baby, and Chevy had told this girl. She knew. This stupid chippy. She *knew!* A turbulence of emotion expanded in Ellen and she had the contrary urges to throw herself sobbing into the girl's arms and at the same time to slap her, hit her and drive her away. A soft-edged putrescence came into her throat but Ellen swallowed it down. She must not throw up. She must not become upset. She began to say the first words that entered her head.

"I noticed you looking at the lamp in the living room," she said, and although the words sounded not at all close to her and not in her own voice, she was amazed at the assurance and confidence they carried.

"Yes," said the girl. "I was."

"That was a gift from my mother-in-law," Ellen said. "It just doesn't fit in the room, does it. It just doesn't balance. I'm going to have to send it back. This is my house, after all, and . . ."

"Well," the girl said. "I'm glad I don't have to say anything nice about it."

"It's a beautiful and expensive piece of furniture," Ellen said. "It just doesn't happen to work with this room. In most houses it would be a complement." She felt in control again, and would perhaps have said more on the subject of the lamp, but at that moment Daniel and Chevy returned from the basement and Ellen, her duty done, left the kitchen.

IV

Daniel was thinking how much his wife had begun to talk like his mother. As long as he had known Ellen she had talked in a low, purring register — a little like Lauren Bacall he had always thought — but now she had added to this the direct and measured and precisioned speech of his mother. At first he had thought that he should point it out to her, but he had decided that there was no real harm in it.

Across the room Ellen was talking now with the foreign student who had come with the bridesmaid, and he was listening to her with terrible intentness, his own lips slightly open as he watched Ellen's lips.

"But that's all so *passé*," Ellen was saying. "Women aren't household domestics any more. A woman's place isn't in the home. In America a woman can be *any*thing. She owes it to herself." The South American looked away, but whether it was in rage or embarrassment Daniel couldn't tell. He had a dark, brooding, passionate, Latin look that made Daniel think he might have a cross under his shirt on a little gold chain.

Daniel smiled and looked away. Yes, she was going to make him a fine little wife. There were things he didn't understand about her, and there were things he didn't even like, but he knew that compatibility was a thing to be achieved. There was no such thing as instant compatibility. Already both of them had adjusted, Daniel thought, a great deal.

He looked again at his wife and then around at his house — so warm and so full of the good sounds of his friends laughing and drinking. Daniel thought that never in his life had he felt so fulfilled. He felt a hand on his shoulder and looked up to see Abe. "Hey," Abe said, "I've been looking around at the house, and I haven't seen the nursery. Where's the nursery going to be?" His eyebrows were raised innocently.

The question had been loud enough to attract the attention of Chevy and his girl as well as Chrystal Morrisey and they all moved a step closer to see how Daniel would handle this. As yet nobody knew about Ellen's pregnancy and therefore everyone suspected.

"Nursery?" Daniel said, blinking a series of bewildered blinks. "Nursery? Nobody sick in my family," he said. Ellen appeared at his elbow and took his arm as if she had come to defend him. "Ellen," he said, "do we need a nur . . ." He had gestured with his drink hand, and it sloshed dangerously.

"Daniel! The rug . . ." Ellen gasped, and then, as if nothing had happened, swept her gaze over her guests. "Does anybody need a drink?" she asked, and then, without waiting for an answer, she began to walk toward the kitchen. Since she still held his arm, Daniel followed.

When they were alone in the kitchen she whirled on him. "What were you telling them out there?" she said. "And what did you tell Chevy?" Daniel saw to his amazement that she was close to tears.

"Tell Chevy? What? When? What's the matter?"

"About us." She touched her stomach briefly with a finger, but her eyes stayed on his.

"Tell? Nothing! My God, Ellen, I wouldn't . . ."

"Well, then how does that chippy know?"

"Who? Chippy? Who?"

"That girl Chevy brought."

"She can't," Daniel said. "It's impossible."

Ellen started to cry, pressing her fists against her mouth, and Daniel folded her in his arms. "You're just nervous. Don't be nervous. The party is going wonderfully and you're a fine hostess." She remained stiff and unyielding in his arms. "Look," he said. "Tomorrow we'll be away from everything. This has been a long, hard, frustrating affair from the beginning. We're going to do nothing but rest and relax and be alone with each other and get to know each other." He was rocking her gently in his arms, crooning. "Just you and me and the birds and the wind and the sky and . . ."

"What?" she said. She stiffened again in his arms. "Daniel," she said sharply. "Where are you taking me?" It was asked in a way that would not admit a playful answer.

"Well," he said, "I guess I can tell you now." He released her and grinned widely. "Mom's got a friend who's got a cabin in the mountains outside Jackson Hole, Wyoming. Ten days with just you and me and . . ."

"Wyoming!" she said. She stared at him unbelievingly. "You said *New York!*"

"No, I didn't, honey. I didn't say . . ."

"Oh, no!" She drew away and her knuckles came up to her mouth again. "Oh, God, Daniel, I've told everybody we're going to New York!"

"Honey," he reached to put his hands on her shoulders. "I don't want to go sightseeing on our honeymoon, I want to get to know . . ."

"Wyoming!" she said, and she whipped around, spilling his hands. "What's in Wyoming?" Great round sobs began to come from her, and Daniel, although he again took her in his arms, knew that he was not welcome. Then, just as the sobs threatened to get out of control, they were over. She straightened and moved away from him into the living room. "Don't say anything to anyone," she said. "Don't you dare tell anyone."

"I've already told Chevy and Abe," he said.

When she heard this she stopped and turned back to

him. "I won't go," she said, and she turned and went into the living room.

Daniel stayed where he was for a moment, watching her leave him, then with stiff and uncertain steps he moved after her. "Ellen!" he said. "Hey!"

She tried to lose him by slipping between two guests, a short-cut route to the bedroom where she could lock the door on him, and when he tried to follow he bumped someone and heard a crash and a series of gasps. He turned to see that Chevy's girl had dropped her drink. The glass had broken and the ice cubes sat in the middle of a dark stain on the rug. For a second no one moved, then Chevy's girl started for the kitchen.

"Is there a cloth out there?" she asked. "I'll get a cloth." She looked very upset and Daniel felt responsible.

"Don't worry," he said with a little laugh. "It's okay."

"*Okay!* Daniel, it's our new *rug!*" It was Ellen, her voice moving toward a new, all-consuming hysteria.

Chevy's girl had paused near the kitchen door. "Is there a cloth?" she asked again. No one answered and after another second she continued into the kitchen and the sound of drawers opening was heard. There was a short, loud shriek from Ellen.

"Don't you touch my kitchen!" she said. "Stay out of my kitchen, you . . . you *chippy!*" She ran the few steps and disappeared after Alberta.

Daniel looked uncertainly after her and then knelt and began to pick up the glass fragments and the ice cubes.

"I bumped into her," he explained. "My fault. Ellen's a little upset."

Chevy's girl exited from the kitchen, her round eyes

rounder, looking at nothing, and after a moment Ellen followed her, a sponge in her hand. Ellen knelt and began to dab at the floor. Daniel knelt beside her.

"Ellen," he said softly but with sternness. "You've got to apologize for that."

"I won't."

"You've got to," he said. He spoke as softly as he was able, but he knew that he was being heard by everyone in the room. "You must," he said.

With a quick, well-coordinated movement Ellen threw the sponge into his face, rose, and without a sound ran again toward the bedroom. In the silence that followed, the sound of her locking the door was very clear.

People began to rearrange themselves, moving into the groups with whom they had arrived, looking seriously at places on the four walls and on the floor.

"She'll be all right," Daniel said with what he knew was too much good humor. "She's been working hard on this wedding and the party and all. Weddings take a lot out of a girl. She'll be back in a minute." He waved his arms. "Everybody. Have another drink. Here, let me mix you another drink." He held out his hands, but people had begun to set their glasses down, assuring Daniel that they had really had enough.

Chrystal Morrisey moved toward the bedroom door. "Ellen?" she called. "Ellen, honey, it's me. Let me in."

There was no answer.

"Ellen, honey? It's me, Chrystal."

Silence.

"Ellen, our *coats* are in there!"

Behind the bedroom door there was a sound of movement, a click of the lock, and then the coats began to fly out the open door, their empty sleeves flapping in astonishment.

The party was over.

THE HONEST HUCKSTER

Chevy was drinking the last of his morning's pot of coffee and reading when he heard below him the final strains of the doxology. Feet scraped outside his door as the choir rose to leave, and he could hear the switches being turned off on the organ. What Chevy did not expect to hear was the knock on his door, and before he could spring to his feet to straighten the room, the hand that had knocked had turned the knob and opened the door.

It was Alberta. She carried in one hand a large brown kite and in the other a heavy-looking paper sack, and from the expression on her face it appeared that she would begin immediately to speak of pleasant things.

Chevy said nothing for a moment. He listened briefly to the sounds below him and then looked at Alberta as if one or the other did not, could not exist.

"Alberta," he said finally in a high and choked voice. "There are people still in this church." He threw the book he had been reading across the room and onto the bed. "Goddamn it," he said, "I could lose my job."

She set the kite in a corner and walked to the bed, still holding the sack, beginning to grin. "I'm really sorry, no kidding, but I forgot all about church being on Sunday. Really, hey. They were all praying or something because it was quiet and I just walked right in. "But . . ." she looked pleased with herself, ". . . when I saw what was happening, I found myself a seat and tried to look like a sinner."

"My God, in bluejeans and with a *kite?*" Chevy almost strangled with the word.

She nodded gaily. "I was getting away with it too, till they brought that plate around for the money . . . and all I had was this sack of bananas and cheeseburgers, and so . . ."

"Did you . . . you didn't . . . did you?" He raised a hand to cover his eyes.

She began to chuckle. "What do you think they'd have done?" she asked. "I mean can you picture these guys, sober as anything, carrying this cold ol' cheeseburger up to the altar and the ol' preacher . . ."

"Alberta, I asked you not to come to the church till services were over. I asked!" He began to swear softly to himself.

"I didn't come to see you," she said lightly. "I came to see Jesus." She held her arms wide. "Give me your weak, your poor, your huddled masses, yearrrrrrning to breathe free . . ."

"That's not Jesus," Chevy said. "That's the fucking Statue of Liberty."

"Chong," said Alberta with a shrug. "Anyway it was kind of sweet. Little old ladies were just smiling at me to beat the band. Most of the time little old ladies look at me like they think I go around strangling kittens or something." She ferreted briefly in her sack. "Wanna banana?" she asked.

"What did you do with the kite. I'll bet you sat right there rattling . . ."

She had begun to peel her banana casually. "There was some guy standing by the door just on the inside, and when I came in he looked kind of nervous and didn't know what to do, so I gave it to him."

"Gave him the kite? Just handed it to him?"

Alberta nodded, watching her banana as if preoccupied with it, but unable to keep from smiling.

"What'd he do?" Chevy closed his eyes and pressed his fingers over them.

"He said 'thank you' and he didn't smile or anything. Just like he did it every Sunday, and when everything was over he was right there with it to give it back." She finished the banana and made a push-shot with the peel toward Chevy's metal, institutional wastebasket. There was a satisfying ring as it went in. "I didn't give him my sack though," she said, chuckling with her mouth full of banana. It was clear that she was entirely pleased with her conduct.

"Oh, Jesus," Chevy said, "it must have been old Angusson. Did the same guy pass the collection plate?"

Alberta nodded.

"Oh, Jesus." Chevy again covered his eyes.

"He's kind of a neat old guy."

"He's one of the people who hired me," Chevy said,

trying without notable success to control his voice. "He can also fire me."

This information had no visible effect on Alberta, and before the echo of it had died from the room Chevy was embarrassed at having brought it up. He covered his eyes again. "Oh, folks," he said, "it's all over. Three golden years under the gentle wing of mother church, and now, just when I'm about to get the light — when I'm on the very verge of a total commitment, I'm torpedoed by a kite-flying wench. Oh, shit," he said. "Whatever will I do?"

Alberta looked at him without expression.

"Well," he said, "I'll just have to resign myself to my fate. No more to hear the golden voice of Billy D. through my walls."

"He's kind of neat too," Alberta offered.

"Billy D.?"

"He's the preacher, isn't he? Yeah, he's kind of neat. He just smiles away when he's talking about ol' Jesus. Just so happy. He's kind of cute."

Chevy was filled with an unexpected jealousy for Billy D. "Oh," he said. "He's happy all right. When Billy D.'s got a mouthful of clichés and an audience that can't ask any questions Billy D.'s got no need for heaven. But you ought to see him, by God, when he comes in *here!* Billy D.'s not so cute in the company of questions. One time . . ."

"It was kind of sweet, though," Alberta interrupted conversationally. "Don't you ever go?"

"Folks, the girl wants to know if I'm ever seen in church. Now I ask . . ."

"C'mon! Do you?"

"Now and again. Often enough to keep Billy D. and Angusson on the line."

"But everybody knows the words to everything and they don't have to wonder about what to do. Everybody just singing the songs all together really solemn. It was sweet. There was this guy across the aisle, and when everybody would stand up for a special prayer or something he'd stand up on his tiptoes because his wife was taller than he was. That's really sad, isn't it. I mean that's really a sad thing to do in church."

"I guess he's just as short in church as any place else," Chevy said. It had an appealing enigmatic ring to it, and Chevy expected her to grin at him, but instead she appeared to be deciding whether or not to agree.

"So!" Chevy said. He left the chair and walked to the kite. "You're gonna tell me next you want me to fly this thing?"

"Sure, I built it specially. Oh! I forgot to tell you. They put new linoleum in Beanie's, and the guys left these little strips of wood, and so I got the idea to make a kite. I haven't made one . . ." she squinted, thinking, ". . . in a hell of a long time."

Chevy saw that it was covered with waxed butcher's paper and had a tail of heavy, white cloth which he realized must be from one of Beanie's aprons. The slender sticks had been carefully carved by hand.

"I haven't tried it yet," she said. "C'mon!"

"You really want to fly a kite? Today?"

"Sure. Picnic!" She shook the sack. "Lunch!"

Then she held the kite over her head and ran the few steps across the room, testing how it took the wind. She lowered it finally and looked seriously at it, considering. "I think it'll fly," she said.

NOW!

It was one of those instants that hold for moments longer than the clock time it consumes — where breath ceases, falling objects suspend, sound forgets to move and an unexpected voice in the mind shouts — commands, NOW! NOW! At such commands unplanned curses are shouted, hands are clenched and swung, peacefully whittling knives slash and plunge, grown sons are grasped and embraced by fathers — in moments such as these marriages are proposed and broken and sometimes women are taken and held with force great enough to crush kites.

Then, "Hurry," she said, "the wind's dying." And Chevy, who had not shouted or leaped or cursed or held, got to his feet and followed her out of the church.

II

Alberta would hear of no other place to fly the kite than at the Promenade, a large, green, open area which centered the campus of Easton like a small hole in a large doughnut. The Easton Chamber of Commerce invariably included a color picture of this park in their brochure, and the picture showed huge, horny-limbed, ancient trees. Under these trees, circling the open area, wove a cobblestone walk. The grass in the area was close-cropped enough and thick enough for golfers to practice on its surface, and when Chevy and Alberta entered the area carrying the kite and sack two men were swinging at perforated plastic balls. The benches under the trees were full of people who would rather, for their own private reasons, be here than anywhere else on this Sunday, the Fourth of July.

Within the circle of trees the greenness was broken at its center by a massive stone, brought in and erected at great expense after the Second World War, which held a bronze plaque on its side giving token to the school's war dead. Under this stone Alberta dropped the sack and took off her shoes and stood for a moment in the grass — eyes glazed and lips curved with pleasure, wiggling her toes in the coolness of the grass. Already the July sun was hot and thick in the sky, seeming several times its normal size and intensity, and except for the golfers, Chevy and Alberta were the only ones not taking advantage of the shade under the trees.

Alberta took the kite, and, letting the string out slowly, ran with it, Chevy following. There was still a slight uncertain breeze, and the kite rose with promise to a respectable height, following gracefully and delicately, but when she stopped, it lost its life and dropped. Several times she made alterations, explaining the aerodynamics of these adjustments carefully while Chevy squatted beside her. Then she would be off again, her helmet of hair bouncing and flying.

She did not, Chevy noticed, run like a girl, with elbows close to the ribs and with wrists winging loosely; and she ran not like a man either with deliberate and muscular strides, but rather like something else that leaped on slender limbs with breathtaking, casual agility — like certain Negro basketball players, able to hang impossibly long in the air between steps. The tails of her shirt pulled free and her bare feet flashed as Chevy padded behind her panting and foolish.

"Not enough wind," she gasped finally, and dropped to the grass under the monument as if she'd been hit by a cannonball. "There'll be some later maybe."

"No," Chevy said, his legs watery and his breath short. He remained standing, one arm against the monument. "Afternoons . . . are always still. Winds start . . . when it cools. In the evenings . . ." he panted ". . . and in the mornings. Change of temperature does it. Never a wind . . . when it's this hot." The uniqueness of the kite flying had left him and he was very aware of the eyes of those who sat on the benches. "Hell," he said. "Let's go."

"Let's wait and see. I think there'll be a wind." Still lying there on her back she gave him the sly look of someone who has access to mystic knowledge, then she closed her eyes and slowly tilted her face into the sun in an unexpectedly lovely and delicate movement. Her face relaxed and her lips parted slightly, and although there was now no breeze at all, a piece of her hair began to flutter and blow on her forehead. Chevy sat, putting his back to the monument and watched as she wrinkled her nose and brought a hand to brush at her face, then he turned from her and reached with an impatient gesture into his pocket. He thumbed two tablets from the roll, and as he chewed them he fished for a cigarette. He turned his head to watch a young man and a young woman sitting on one of the benches under the trees. The two were looking at each other quietly, their only movement the slowly knotting fingers of the hands which they had extended across the space between them. Chevy and Alberta had walked by them with the kite on the way to the monument, and the lovers were still in the same posture as they had been then, as if part of the Promenade's statuary — something entitled, Chevy thought, "True Love," and commissioned by the Easton Federation of Women's Clubs. He felt oppressed by the heat, and he envied them their bench and their shade and their ability to stare mindlessly into each other's blank eyes. He began to think about Daniel, married less than twenty-four hours.

"Hey," he said, not loudly.

Alberta opened one eye, bringing up a hand to shade it, peering at him.

"Forgot to tell you. Daniel and I planned that when he and Ellen got back we'd all go camping together. Just the four of us. Live in a tent for a couple weeks."

"Oh, yeah?"

"Yeah. And every day ol' Daniel and me'd go fishing. You two — you and ol' Ellen — you could have a big time playing games and stuff."

"I can hardly wait," Alberta said, unblinking. "Play throw the ol' sponge."

"I thought you might go for the idea."

Alberta snickered and closed the eye again. Then after a moment she opened it and rose to one elbow. "Really, though," she said, "I've been thinking about her. Remember when you asked me how come I didn't like college?

What was the thing that turned me off most? Well, she's it. For example . . ." Alberta sat up and crossed her legs Indian-style ". . . for example, in this English class I had some graduate student for special discussions twice a week. Now these people are enough to finish you off all by themselves, but anyway everybody in the class was just like Ellen — girls and guys. I remember once we spent about a whole hour doing nothing but discussing how to pronounce Karamazov, like in the *The Brothers Kara — Karama* — but for about an hour everybody sat around getting really intense about it and looking sensitive and oh, shit!"

"Karamazov," pronounced Chevy, unable to stop himself.

Alberta did not notice. "I'll tell you what," she said. She tilted her head, sighting at nothing in particular. "She's the kind of person that when you send her to the store for jelly, she'll come back with grape every time. Every time!"

Chevy had been preparing something to say, but now he just blinked, reviewing this.

"I kind of like ol' Daniel though," she said, and for no reason she smiled a huge pleased smile. "Have you ever thought of getting married?" she asked.

"Huh?" In an instant he managed to smile, but he wondered what his initial expression had shown her.

"Married. Married," she said. "You know? Have you ever thought it might be sweet?"

"Well," Chevy said in measured and modulated tones, not looking at her, "it's occurred to me."

"Well, every time it starts to sound good to me — you

know, when I see too many movies or something like that — the thing to do is to go visit some married guys. That turns me off like a cold shower." She snapped her fingers to show how fast.

"Yeah," Chevy said, and turned back to the couple on the bench, his heart thumping unaccountably and even for the July sun suddenly perspiring too much. After a minute he spoke. "Hot," he said.

"Sundays are always sunny. Did you ever notice that?" She had lain back down, but now she opened and shaded one eye again.

"Not always," he said.

"Well, not *al*ways, but there're more sunny Sundays than other days."

"Oh, God, Berta. There are not. It's just that you notice Sunday more because it's your day off." He was very annoyed, and he didn't know why.

"No." she said. "It was that way when I was a kid too. Really."

"Sundays were still your day off, because you were in school the rest of the time." It had been only by effort that he had not allowed the annoyance to enter his voice.

"You've always got *rea*sons for everything," Alberta said. She closed her eye.

"Well, what are your conclusions? That God sends more sun on Sunday?"

"See," she said, her eyes still closed. "It's even called *Sun*-day."

"No more church for you, Berta." He was controlling himself admirably, managing even to smile in her direction. "You're starting to talk like Billy D."

"You're starting to talk like a man with a paper asshole," she informed him.

After a second he sighed audibly. "What have you got against logic, Berta? C'mon. Out with it. You've got a real deep-seated mistrust of anything that makes sense, don't you."

"You're always making sense," Alberta said in an insulting way.

"I try to," he said, and bitterness colored his words. "I try to make sense, and I try like hell to be clear and consistent and honest and truthful . . ." The awareness that he was lying grew, but the words did not stop, ". . . but it's damned hard when nobody listens — nobody pays any attention."

"Yes," Alberta began, "somebody listens very carefully to every damned . . ."

"Like hell!" he said, leaning suddenly toward her from the monument. "Let me try to be serious with you for a minute. Let me try to be logical and you aren't even listening."

"Right," Alberta said. "But *you* are. The minute you stop listening so hard, I'll start. Okay?"

She lay back again and covered her eyes with her arm, and Chevy stared at her for several long, tense seconds. Then his own eyes closed and he relaxed, leaning his head back against the stone. After a moment he lit another cigarette, smoking it through although it tasted black and unhealthy. He brought his eyes again to the bench where sat the hand-holding lovers, and as he watched, the two rose and began to walk the cobblestones, still holding hands. They were in full profile to Chevy, walking slowly and without excessive energy in the heat, and as Chevy watched them the man seemed suddenly shaped in an odd and familiar way — his thick, sagging limbs and trunk bringing to mind after a second the picture in some long-ago biology book of a bulging and unhealthy-looking man, naked and in profile, labeled "endomorph." Chevy remembered his child's pride in the fact that he looked more like the picture of the "normal," the mesomorph.

He turned away and closed his eyes and waited for wind. The endomorph would know just what to do with his hand-holding companion, he thought. He'd propose to her, not on bended knee, probably, but with the proper, the acceptable words and gestures and expressions, and he'd take her home to mother and father just as if he'd been a normal. He'd get married to her, knowing exactly what to do, and he'd have children.

Chevy opened his eyes and looked for Alberta, but she had moved from the place where she had been lying and was now on her hands and knees, moving slowly and watching something with great intensity. She was, he realized after a moment, following the progress of an ant.

"Hey!" he said, just to fill the breathless air with a sound, "What'cha doin'?"

She raised a hand in acknowledgment, but didn't lift her eyes. "Man," she said in a loud slow whisper, as if afraid of frightening something. "This crazy bastard's got a piece of grass about the size of a fence post, and he's . . ." she paused to watch, her mouth a little parted and then, the crisis past, began to crawl again; after a moment Chevy realized that he had been forgotten. He opened his shirt another button and blotted his forehead. The air around him and her and all the air inside the circle of still trees seemed hot and heavy and portentous, like that in a breath-blown paper bag before the hands close upon it. Chevy took several deep lungfuls of air, gathering strength before finally, and with great effort, he brought himself to his feet and walked to where she was.

"How's he doin'?" he said.

It was not the kind of question that demands an answer, and without looking at him or speaking, she reached out and slipped her grass-cool hand under his pant cuff and gripped it around his ankle. He squatted beside her.

"Did it ever strike you, Miss Raynes," he said, "as it just did me, that our parent generation is as different from us as the larva from the pretty butterfly?" The cool, brief hand on his ankle had exhilarated him, and he was speaking in a grand, stagy pose. "Has it struck you yet," he orated, "that evolution took a giant step between them and us?"

"Nope," she said. Then, after a moment, "How'd you like to be an ant?"

She had probably not even heard him. "I mean," Chevy said, still grandly — more grandly — determined to get her attention. ". . . I mean the problem is that before anybody, least of all us airy butterflies, figured out that we weren't going to be larvae forever, they taught us all the rules and codes and processes of the larva, see?" He was on his haunches, sidling along beside her.

"Rules and codes, Boy!" Alberta said. She crawled

along shaking her head with great seriousness, and Chevy behind and beside her, smiled a little to himself and shook his own head. He decided to drive this metaphor to its ultimate absurdity. He would continue until she realized that she had not been listening properly — not listening at all. A little object lesson for Alberta.

"The stuff that works for butterflies isn't the same as that which works for larvae," he said. "It just doesn't apply. But the ol' larvae, they won't even admit that we're different. They want us to be larvae too. They think that's all there is."

"Mmmmm," said Alberta.

Chevy moved more to the front of her, determined to get her attention. "But the world turned clear over between them and us," he said tragically. "Turned clear over. Evolution took a giant step. The problem is that all those pretty butterflies are going to get convinced that they really are larvae after all. Don't you think so?"

"That's right! Damn right! Hey, move will you? He's coming your way."

"They'll lose their wings," Chevy continued, thoroughly enjoying himself now, having almost forgotten the lesson he had in mind. "If nothing else, Alberta," he said, his voice trembling, a finger jabbing theatrically at the sky, "we mustn't lose our wings. How to learn to live with them, that's our challenge — our purpose! How to overcome our larva training, that's our cross! We mustn't lose our wings." He expected her to turn to him at this point, and he covered his face with a Nathan Hale expression of gravity and high purpose. She turned to him.

"We won't lose them," she said. "I don't think you

should worry about that." Her large green eyes, he saw to his dismay, were serious. She had missed it again, and Chevy knew in an instant that there was no hope of convincing her that it had all been a fine joke, and one at her expense at that. There was nothing to do but to try to salvage it as serious.

"Berta," he said, behind her again, his voice now low and serious. "What I mean is — is — what I want you to understand is that many people — *most* people have that problem. Do you see?" The crease had appeared between his eyes and his hands were twisting grass. "Even people who seem like they don't have them, they have the same problems. It's only by work, by damned hard work, that they manage to keep it from having too much effect on their lives and actions, do you see? People are either trying to learn what it is to be, you know, to be a damned butterfly, and that's a terrible problem — are you listening to me?"

"Sure! Sure!" She took her eyes from the ground.

". . . or else they're trying to please everybody else by being a larva and they wind up . . ."

"Me? Do you mean me?" She was not insulted, only interested.

"Not you, Berta, I mean people! Everybody! I mean it's the condition of things for people of our generation, do you see?"

"No," she said, but it didn't seem to bother her. She looked back to find her ant. "There you are, you little son-of-a-bitch," she said.

"Well, Alberta, what I mean — what I want you to see . . ." he stopped and fumbled a tablet from the roll in his pocket, ". . . is that it's difficult for people to be consistent under these conditions, so you have to make allowances. Don't judge a person by his consistency."

The grass was gone from his hands, and he began to look severely toward the bench where the endomorph had sat with his girl, knowing abjectly that he hadn't made sense, knowing that he hadn't even managed to make his words seem important. He began to collect saliva in his mouth to make the crushed pill easier to swallow. His mouth was very dry.

"I don't judge people," Alberta said, looking up again.

"Yes, you do," he said. "You judged Ellen."

"I didn't *judge* her, I just don't like the bitch," Alberta said calmly. She left her knees and sat on her haunches in order to look more formally involved and concerned with the problem which she now saw disturbed Chevy a great deal. "Well," she said when he didn't answer, "*maybe* I judged her. How do you not judge people?"

"Oh, I don't know. We're way the hell off the subject."

"What subject?" Alberta said. She slapped her knee and grinned. "I never did . . ."

"Oh, nothing," he said. "Go ahead with what you were doing. Go find your ant. First things first." Chevy felt harried and cornered, and he was not able to keep this from showing clearly in his voice.

"That's okay," she said without particular emphasis. "You probably stepped on him anyway." She got up and began to move back toward the monument. Chevy followed.

"Oh, I'm sorry," he said finally. He put both hands in his back pockets and walked beside her, watching his feet move through the grass. "I'm not making any damn sense. I've got a lot on my mind."

"What?"

"What to *do!*" he exploded. "What'll we *do,* Berta? I've got to get the hell out of this town! My life is starting to repeat itself! I'm starting to develop patterns that scare the hell out of me! Let's just go!" He gestured violently with one arm in no direction, wishing as soon as the words were out that he could have said it differently — with less heat, wondering why he hadn't. He had not wanted to say it that way at all. He wanted it to be exciting — spontaneous. But then he had been disappointing himself quite a bit during the past few weeks.

"Okay," Alberta said, her eyes still on the grass, "let's go."

"Where?" he said, empty and sick with himself.

"Oh, let's do go to New York. I'm just dying to see Broadway again." She sucked in her cheeks, speaking in an intense whisper.

"Seriously!" Chevy said. "Just for five minutes be serious with me today, okay?" They had reached the monument and they sat under it although the area of shade had diminished considerably.

"Is there any place?" Chevy continued, ". . . any place at all where you'd like to go? Seriously! I'm ready for anything. Let's do something spectacular. Let's do the thing that everybody wants to do but never does."

"Really?"

"Yeah."

"*Really?*" Alberta started to smile an excited smile.

"Yeah, sure, really."

"Hey then, I know. I've got something I've always wanted to do." Then she looked away and wrinkled her nose. "Aw, you wouldn't want to," she said.

"Sure I would. What? What is it?"

". . . and we could stop along the way and earn money if we needed it."

"What?"

Alberta had cocked her head as if listening to a distant whisper. "Yeah!" she said, her smile growing. "I don't know why we couldn't."

"Do you mind . . ."

"Follow the Lewis and Clark Trail. Chevy, let's do it. Start from Mandan, North Dakota, and across the Rockies like they did and come out on the Columbia. This ranch we used to have where I almost got the horse was right on this river where they went, and I read the *Journals* and even found some of the places they talked about. Oh, man . . ."

"Are you serious?" He had moved his head out of the area of shade toward her in order to see her better.

"Sure. We could do it this summer. We could start right away." She put a thumbnail between her teeth and closed one eye and began to figure. "We'd need good walking boots," she murmured, ". . . and back-packs."

"Alberta," he was almost laughing. "Jesus, you can't be serious."

She looked at him for a long minute, then she took the thumbnail from her mouth. "Chevy," she said in a very patient way, "what did you have in mind? Take a tour some place? Feed the fucking bears?"

"Well . . ." He looked away from her with a pained expression. "C'mon . . ." he said. "I don't mean an expedition. I mean a place! A place where you can live and where there'd be an opportunity for self-actualization, you know? Where you could live and just learn to be what you are."

"Learn-to-be-what-you-are," she repeated in the voice of a stage dummy.

"Don't play word games, Berta, for Christ's sake. I'm trying to be serious. Can't you see that?"

"Does it have to be a place?"

"Sure it does. I don't want to *do*. I want to *be*. Our parent generation, they were the *do*ers, and it's up to us to *be*. It isn't necessary to do any more. Don't be taken in by all this *do* crap."

She didn't answer this, but appeared to be thinking about it with great difficulty. "Are you sure you have to be in a special place in order to be?" she asked. "I mean a person has to do something anyway, so why not do something you want to do while you're being, see?"

"Alberta," he said wearily. "Not the Lewis and Clark Trail, okay?" He took another cigarette, lit it, and Alberta watched until he had blown out a long lungful of smoke.

"How about the fair?" she said.

"The fair?"

"Join the fair. There's a fair coming here sometime around Labor Day. I saw the posters. There's going to be a rodeo too. I was going to invite you to go to that with me." She moved around and placed herself in front of him, becoming excited again. "But hey! Let's go with the fair when it comes." She held her hand in front of her mouth, gripping a microphone. *"Step right up, lay-dees and gents,"* she began in a nasal voice. *"See the lizard boy! It walks it talks and it crawls on its belly like a rep-tile!"*

"Would you really like to do that kind of thing?" he asked after a moment, not smiling at all.

"What kind of thing?"

"Exploit some poor freak? Take advantage of people? Do you want to involve yourself with that kind of sham and pretense? Are you trying to tell me that that would be a good place to get self-actualized?" He could not look at her. He was painfully aware that he was being petty and niggling and small, but there seemed to be no alternative. He felt trapped and oppressed. He began to undo the rest of the buttons of his shirt.

"Well, *you* wouldn't have to be dishonest, would you?"

"You'd be involved," he insisted, looking at something under the circle of trees.

There was a silence of some seconds during which one of the golfers swung at and hit one of the perforated balls with a dry empty sound.

"I don't think it's all dishonest," Alberta said, and Chevy was aware that she had taken a stand, that the total or partial dishonesty of fairs had been challenged and must be defended to a decision. This kind of confrontation had occurred only a few times between them, and Chevy had found Alberta a determined and a willful opponent. Now, in the heat, he did not feel up to the dispute. The sun was directly overhead and there was no shade under the monument.

"I suppose you're right," he said wearily. "It's not all dishonest."

"Well then?" she continued doggedly.

"You're right! You're right!" They were not looking at each other. "But I'd prefer not to involve myself in it anyway."

"In the first place," she said, a little louder than normal, "some people do have fun. Not everybody runs around with some big wrinkle between their eyes."

"You're right, Berta, okay? Let's drop it. This is goofy. We manage to have the dumbest arguments."

"Well, hey there, Ulysses, what kind of an adventure did you have in mind?"

He decided to let this pass in partial payment for the smallness and the injustice of his recent objections. He even managed to laugh a laugh that showed he was aware of his guilt. "We could go down south and join some civil rights group, I suppose." He was pleased that he had managed to make this sound almost enthusiastic.

"Count me out," Alberta said. "I saw what they're doing to the Indians back home. Now *that's* exploitation. *That's* what dishonesty is, boy!" Again, although she was baiting him, he did not object.

"We could join the Peace Corps as a team, maybe." Again, a near enthusiasm.

"Wouldn't we have to be married? I don't think they like unmarried teams. That wouldn't be bad, though," she said. "That would be kind of sweet. Do you think they have a big call for waitresses?"

Chevy tried hard to laugh. "What would be sweet?" he asked. "You mean getting married?"

"No, I mean Peace Corps."

"Yeah, we'd have to be married all right," he said casually.

"Yeah," she said. "We could do that. That would be pretty spectacular and different."

"Ha ha," said Chevy again. Then after a moment, coolly, "You want to?"

"What?"

"Get married?"

"I don't know," she said. "Do *you* want to? I hadn't exactly given it a lot of thought."

"No, I don't," he said, grinning at her, his hands tearing up another handful of grass. He knew he should say more to take the curse of seriousness from it, but he could think of nothing. He could tell her eyes were on him.

"What do you mean?" she said.

"Mean?"

"Something's on your mind," she said.

"Well, dammit!" He threw the grass in the air in a despairing, angry movement. "What the hell are we going to do with ourselves? I don't want to get married either, but what are we going to do then?"

"Do?" she said, baffled.

"Do! Do! That's why I wanted to go some place."

"I thought you said you wanted to *be!* I thought you said you didn't want to do."

"Alberta," he said. He was perspiring, and he took his shirt tail and brushed his forehead angrily. "You are just impossible to talk to. Quit trying to trip me up. Why does it give you such pleasure to trip me up? Ask yourself that. Just try to communicate with me, okay?"

"Boy," she said. "You can really be ob-goddamn-noxious sometimes, fella. You know that?"

"Let's not fight." He held both his hands toward her like a policeman. "I don't want to fight on Sundays. It's our only damned day out of the whole . . ."

"Chevy, you *said* you didn't want to *do!* You *said* it!"

"Let's not quibble. What I'd like to know is what about you? Are you just content to go on doing what we're doing now?"

She considered this. "Well, I could get Beanie to let me work mornings instead of nights. He wouldn't like it much, but . . ."

"That's not what I mean. I mean in our lives. What do we do now? What next?"

"Next?" she said with a troubled look. "Next?"

Then there was another moment where the unexpected voice commanded *now!* and this time Chevy obeyed. "Yes, next!" he shouted. "Or do we go nowhere from here? Do we peter off and you find yourself somebody else to sleep with and I wait to get drafted. Yes, next!"

Someone hit another perforated golf ball before Alberta began to speak. "I'm going to try to explain something to you," she said. "I'm going to have to explain it because you're so goddamned dumb that you can't . . ."

"I'm sorry," he said abjectly.

"You sure as shit are," she said.

"I really am," he said.

"I know it," she said. "Now listen. You pretend to know so much about fairs. Well did you ever notice the guy who sells things — just sells things out behind the tents? Sometimes there is just one guy with watches or potato peelers or lint removers or something, and sometimes there are guys with wagonloads of different things with assistants and everything. Anyway, they get a big crowd of people, and . . ."

"Hucksters," Chevy said, eager to show that he was paying attention.

"What?"

"Hucksters."

"Well, whatever they are they stand there and sell watches for seven-fifty and say that they're supposed to really cost about twenty-five dollars. Anyway, I'm the guy who buys all that stuff. I'm the one guy who's always right in there with seven-fifty. I sent for this television set once when I was a kid with some box tops, and . . ."

"Something for nothing. They attract people who think they can . . ."

"But the one thing I used to wonder," Alberta continued as if he had not said a word, ". . . was why people did it. I didn't even know why I did it. I didn't need any lint remover, did I? Hell no."

"Something for nothing," Chevy began again eagerly, "Everybody . . ."

"I don't think so, because most of the people knew they were probably going to pay money and wind up with nothing, so how come?" She sighted at him and raised her shoulders to show that it was a puzzling question. "I mean, I watched, and it was the same people going from one of these guys to the other buying lint removers and watches and potato peelers till . . ."

"Why did they do it then?"

She opened her mouth and held it that way for a moment and her face went blank. "I'm damned if I know," she murmured. Her eyes were blank with amazement. "I thought I knew. I thought I knew why."

"They figure they're going to get something out of it for themselves," Chevy said.

Alberta had clenched her teeth on her thumbnail again. "But it isn't the thing," she said. "It isn't the thing that they want."

"What thing?"

"The *thing* — the potato peeler or watch or whatever. That isn't the thing they want out of it. I don't think they want anything like that."

"What else is there? How can they not want anything?"

"Well, look. I mean who needs a potato peeler? It isn't any damned po*ta*to peeler. It's like when a guy comes into Beanie's and says 'gimme a hamburger steak.' Now he's gotta believe that he's gonna get a hamb steak, doesn't he? I mean if he goes around not ordering because he's afraid he's gonna get horse meat, then he's gonna get awfully damned hungry. Besides insulting Beanie."

Chevy drew air between his teeth noisily as if the reasoning of this gave him genuine pain.

"Okay, okay," he said. She was waving her hands all around now and talking very loud. "Okay. It's a crummy example. But the thing is that the guy selling those things really figures he's got all the people conned. He figures that these people are really one born every minute and all that. Listen!" She was really shouting now, her eyes huge with outrage. "Some guy asks people to trust him, and some people do it. Who's wrong, the people? Those people know what's *really* going on more than the huckster does! They know what's happening, man!"

"Alberta, I hate to say this, but you're contradicting yourself all over the place."

"Well," she said. She took a deep breath and was suddenly deflated and calm. "It probably wasn't the best example in the world."

"Not a huckster," he agreed.

"But anyway, that's why I did it."

"Did what?" he said after a moment.

She put the tip of her tongue out and touched it to her upper lip, holding it tensely there for a moment as if waiting for something to pass. "You didn't get it, huh?"

"Get what, Alberta? Really, I . . ."

"Well, forget about it then, but one of these days I'm gonna be one."

"Be one what? Jesus, Alberta, try to be . . ."

"An honest one, just to prove you're full of crap." There was less anger in her voice than pure undiluted willfulness.

"An honest huckster? An honest huckster? Alberta, for Christ's sake, that's a cont . . ."

"That's what I'm gonna be next, and all those people like me who come around . . ."

"Alberta . . ." he was laughing, and he tried to put his arms around her, but she pulled away. "You can't be . . ."

"Well, I don't care how hard it is," she said. "That's what I'm gonna be next, and when I do I'll let you know so you can come and see."

He was still laughing, unable to help himself, and she watched him laugh, not judging and not participating—not angry, but if anything amused by it. She reached calmly into the sack they had brought and pulled out another banana and started to peel it. "Lunch time," she said. She motioned toward the sack, indicating that he should eat.

"An honest huckster," he said. "Folks, did you hear that?" He crawled toward the sack, smiling a grand smile and shaking his head. "Alberta," he said, "you're really wonderful, you know that? You really are something."

"I amuse you, Ulysses? Is that it?"

"When you aren't pissing me off, or confusing me—then yes, you're probably amusing hell out of me." He was not laughing now, and they continued to look at each other, and Chevy abruptly remembered his parents and the Sunday dinner that he was already almost late for, and just that fast he asked Alberta to come home with him for dinner.

"Huh?" she said, the banana poised for another bite.

He repeated the offer.

"To your house? To meet your parents?" A grin began to split her face, and she lowered the banana.

"Sure," he said, not allowing himself to judge or even think about the advisability of the offer.

The grin became wider. "Do I go under an alias?"

"You'll go as Alberta 'Fuck You' Raynes, notorious foulmouth and kite-maker *extraordinaire*."

He was intoxicated by the idea, knowing without thinking about it that it was exactly, precisely the right thing to do.

"Listen," Alberta said. "I'm not exactly the kind of girl friend every mother dreams about for her only son."

"Then fuck mother," Chevy said with a grand wave of his arm, just managing not to crease his forehead.

"This is liable to be more than I can take in one day," she said. "Church in the morning and now this. What can possibly happen tonight?"

III

Mr. Callister's reading glasses were far down on his nose and he peered over them, squinting myopically at the two people who had invaded his home. He did not rise until Chevy and the girl stood directly in front of him and until his son, more belligerent than courteous, made the introduction.

Mr. Callister's blue eyes betrayed nothing more than his own calmness. He repeated her name once as if hearing it for the first time and wishing to fix it in his memory, and he offered Alberta a firm but reserved grip.

"I'm pleased to make your acquaintance, Miss Raynes," he said. "I certainly hope that you've come for dinner."

At that moment Mrs. Callister entered the living room-dining room area with a steaming bowl in each hand. She stopped in mid-stride as if she'd discovered her son and husband being threatened by a gunman who had not yet seen her. Several equally extreme thoughts did occur to her before she realized that Chevy had actually broken a six-year record and had brought a guest home to dinner. But Mrs. Callister was possessed of a more quick and pliable mind than either her son or her husband gave her credit for. By the time she was noticed, she had decided what to do.

"Hello, Chevy," she said coolly, depositing the bowls on the table.

"Mother," Chevy said, "I'd like you to meet Alberta Raynes."

"Alberta Raynes," repeated Mrs. Callister, walking toward her. "What a pretty name. I certainly hope you've come for dinner, Miss Raynes."

"Yes, she has." The tone of Chevy's voice carried a hidden question. It showed him to be someone who isn't certain he won't be contradicted.

"How wonderful." Mrs. Callister tilted her head and smiled the smile of someone who is not at all unused to having an unexpected extra at her Sunday table. "I'm always so happy to meet Chevy's friends," she said.

Chevy began to look at his mother as if he were uncertain of her identity.

"Haven't I heard that name before?" Mrs. Callister mused. "Have I met you before, dear?"

"If you'd met anyone as pretty as Miss Raynes before," her husband said gallantly, "I'm certain you'd remember."

Mrs. Callister appropriated this compliment for herself. "I never forget a face," she explained, and as if to show the secret of her powers she began to look closely at Alberta's broken nose, memorizing it, and Alberta, unnerved, brought up a hand which she was able to divert at the last possible moment to her scalp, where it scratched vigorously.

"Whatever have you two been doing?" Mrs. Callister asked when the nose was fixed firmly in her mind. She indicated the grass stains on the knees of Alberta's blue denims, and Alberta, for whom grass stains had always had a specific and particular meaning, began instantly to blush.

"We, aahh . . ." she began. Her runaway hands began to dip toward her knees before being channeled into a huge, leisurely stretch which seemed, after it was done, only to confirm the hint given by the grass stains. "We were on a picnic," Alberta said. ". . . in the Promenade." She appeared to be tremendously relieved that it had been such a public place and that there had been numerous witnesses to their innocence.

"A picnic? Then you won't be hungry." Mrs. Callister tucked her chin toward her chest and looked moderately grieved. "Oh, I'm so sorry," she said.

"But we didn't eat anything," Alberta explained.

"Ohh?" Mrs. Callister was clearly puzzled.

"We, you know . . ." One of Alberta's hands, expanded to look as much like a kite as possible, came up and made two passes through the air in front of her. "We just flew a kite," she said.

"How did you get it up without any wind?" asked Mr. Callister with great interest.

"Well, we didn't actually get it up at all," Alberta said. "But . . . but we tried." Her face spoke a desperate desire to be believed, and her hand came up again and made several labored passes through the air, indicating much exertion with the kite. She noticed Mr. Callister's eyes following the hand, and she brought it down quickly and stored it in one of her armpits.

"Well, well," Mr. Callister said, and he laughed a calm, unhasty, pleasant laugh. "A picnic where nobody eats and a kite-flying where no one flies kites. I guess I'll just never understand this younger generation."

"Shall we?" Mrs. Callister said with a gesture meant to indicate that they should all sit.

The Callister living room was arranged so that it would be possible to seat a committee of eight or so around a very large coffee table. An L-shaped couch offered seating space for about five medium-sized persons, and there were three lounge chairs of different sizes. Somehow Alberta found herself in the elbow of the couch while the three Callisters sat in the three chairs — a small audience. By some ominous coincidence they had all three, mother, father and son, crossed their right leg over their left, their ankles hanging parallel. In Alberta's already over-pressured mind they seemed a panel.

"Alberta made the kite herself," Chevy was saying as they all sat.

"Oh, really?" Mrs. Callister said. "You must be a very athletic girl, Alberta."

"I'm not, really," Alberta said, speaking far too rapidly and knowing it, but unable to even think about how to slow herself. "Anything to do with balls, for example . . . well, I'm just not too good at it." One of her hands escaped her again, and she noticed in horror that she had it extended in front of her — cupped. "Big balls, I mean," she amended, closing the hand and jerking it back toward her lap. "Little balls aren't too bad. I mean little like marbles." The hand came up again and made a flicking motion with the thumb. "I was marbles champion of my whole town when I was in grade school."

All three of her auditors nodded their heads and smiled their pleasure at this news, but none of them seemed to be able to phrase anything sufficiently congratulatory to say about it.

"But I was always getting C's in gym class," Alberta continued, faster now. "I didn't get along with the women gym teachers too great. They all looked like they went around tearing apples in half and things. Ha ha."

"Marbles champion," Mrs. Callister said with a game expression. "Well, well. Isn't that nice." She stood. "Well, I've got to get the rest of the meal on the table. Will you excuse me?" She smiled at Alberta. "I'm always so glad to have Chevy bring home friends for Sunday dinner. We always have so much fun."

Chevy looked after her as she walked away, his eyes unbelieving.

Mr. Callister began to tap his fingers rapidly against his kneecap in a shave-and-a-haircut-six-bits rhythm.

"Well," he said with an air of authority, as though satisfied with the execution of an earlier command, "It's hot!"

"Yes, it is," Chevy affirmed. He had unobtrusively taken the roll of tablets from his pocket and was now attempting to dislodge two of them without attracting attention to himself, but since it was the only motion in the room, both his father's and Alberta's eyes followed his progress with interest. When he had placed them, after much fumbling, into his mouth, his father broke the silence.

"Chevy's mother thinks he has an ulcer," he told Alberta, leaning toward her with a hand cupped near his mouth.

"He does," Alberta said. Then, when she observed the look that passed over Chevy's face, she lifted a hand and made a tiny distance between finger and thumb. "But only a little one," she amended.

"I haven't got any ulcer," Chevy said, a mild annoyance in his voice.

"It's a wonder you *all* don't have ulcers," Mr. Callister said, still talking to Alberta. "To grow up in this age — so many problems of choice." He pressed his lips together and looked grave. "In the thirties, choice was easy."

"He never forgets either," Chevy told Alberta with a smile, but she didn't understand.

"But Chevy, I think, is an especially nervous and impatient young man," he said. "It worries me. Too highly strung. Too nervous. Don't you agree, Miss Raynes?"

Miss Raynes nodded that yes, she certainly did agree.

"Oh, hell, I am not," Chevy said as good-naturedly as he was able.

Alberta began to nod, first to Chevy and then to his father with a concerned look on her face. "Yes, you are," she said.

"C'mon, Alberta . . ." Chevy tried to communicate something to her with his eyes, but she did not see. She was talking to her new friend.

"He even gets impatient waiting for electric eye doors to open," she was telling him.

"Oh, Berta, for God . . ."

"I've *seen* you, Chevy. You walk along and step on the mat, and if you even have to slow down you get all up tight."

"Really?" her new friend asked. "Is that a fact?"

This test of veracity was interrupted by Mrs. Callister's re-entry from the kitchen. "Soup's on!" she sang. "Come and get it!" She grabbed the back of a chair and shook it vigorously. "Why don't you sit here, Alberta? Just sit right down and dig right in. It isn't much today. Just kind of a Sunday potluck."

"Oh," Alberta assured her, "It looks great. I'm just ravished." She patted her stomach with a fist.

Nobody seemed able to say anything for several minutes. Plates were loaded and eating begun by everyone except Mrs. Callister, who monitored.

"Have some of these rolls," she said, holding yet another plate toward Alberta.

"Thank you."

Mrs. Callister took the butter dish and placed it near Alberta's plate and continued to watch until the first bite was taken and swallowed. "I'll bet your mother was a good cook, Alberta," she said. "It's clear to me that you are someone who enjoys good food."

Alberta, with her mouth very full, managed an unsteady but workable smile.

"What dish was she best at?" Mrs. Callister asked. She was slowly buttering half of one of her rolls. "What dish do you always think of when you think of her? Gravy? Pie? Roast Chicken? Rolls?"

"She wasn't much of a cook," Alberta said. "Like when

she'd start peeling potatoes, she'd start trying to cut the peel all in one strip or something and forget about supper." Alberta seemed to feel at home with this story. "Actually," she continued, "what I remember Mom best for is oatmeal. We used to have it every morning, and my father'd say, 'Eat it, kid, it'll stick to your ribs.' " She had started this story gaily, but it began to run down somewhat toward the end when it did not appear to gladden the hostess. "Even now," Alberta finished, trying to salvage it by being as serious as possible, ". . . even now I can't look oatmeal in the face."

Mrs. Callister said nothing. She placed a baked potato on her plate and began to saw it slowly in half. "Do you go to the university, Alberta?" she asked.

"I did . . ." Alberta began with her mouth full. She chewed hastily and swallowed with what was obviously great effort and some pain, requiring her to stretch her neck at one point. "I did," she repeated, somewhat out of breath with the effort, "but I don't. Not now. And I don't think I will."

"Her brother is a professional rodeo rider out west," Chevy said quickly with the helpful air of someone offering information which will clear up confusion. "Barebacks and broncs," he said.

"*Brahmas* and bareback," Alberta corrected. "A bareback is a bronc."

No one seemed to know exactly how to react to this information. Mrs. Callister occupied herself with emptying the contents of her baked potato onto her plate. Finally Mr. Callister spoke.

"You aren't from this state, then, is that right, Miss Raynes?"

With a fork in one hand and sitting on the other, Alberta was feeling more controlled. She shook her head that she wasn't and mentioned the name of her home town. "It's just a little dump," she explained.

"I'm sure it isn't," Mrs. Callister said with a smile.

"Yes, it is," Alberta said. "Really!"

Mrs. Callister decided to concede this point. She dropped her eyes and began to mash with her fork the half-potato she had just scooped from the shell. She looked preoccupied and baffled, and after a moment she looked up again.

"Now I just know I've heard your name before, Alberta," she said.

"Eat, Mother," Chevy said. He smiled a massive smile and brought his own fork up to his mouth as if to show her how. His mother continued to look at Alberta.

"You just have the prettiest green eyes, Alberta," she said. "Mine are brown and Mr. Callister's are blue. The chances were very good that Chevy's would be blue too, but they turned out brown." She sighed, the disappointment returning. "He carries blue genes though," she said. "His children might have blue eyes. Are there blue eyes in your family, Alberta?"

Alberta shook her head that there were not, and everyone turned their attention to the center of their plates, mentally evaluating the chances of a blue-eyed issue out of a Chevy-Alberta union.

"Oh!" Mrs. Callister said, sitting up sharply as if she had been stung in the small of the back by an insect.

"Chevy, I meant to ask you, how was the wedding. Daniel's wedding?"

"Folks," Chevy said. "How do you suppose she got from point A to point B in that last stream-of-consciousness sequence? Is that a classic study or not? Now I ask you."

"Well how *was* it?" his mother insisted.

"You mean you didn't hear? Really? Well listen! Lightning split the church in two and in rode four gypsies on black horses. They snatched up the bride and rode away. Then . . ."

Mrs. Callister appeared not to have heard. She was sending fox-like glances from Chevy to Alberta and back again, alert for some signal which could be recognized and interpreted. "I thought it might have given you some ideas," she said.

"I got the idea I'd never get married in a church," Chevy said.

"Oh, you never can tell about that," Mrs. Callister said in a high, sweet sing-song voice women use to tease children. "I'd watch out before I'd make statements like that. Isn't that right, Arnold?"

"Mmmmm," said Mr. Callister without looking up.

"Statements like that have a way of coming back to haunt you," she said, grinning back and forth from one to the other.

Chevy was clearly annoyed. "When I get married, Mother," he said, "you'll be the first to know. I'll bring her right home after the ceremony and introduce her all around."

"Oh, *Chevyyyyy*. You know you'd want a church wedding." Mrs. Callister spoke with confidence. "Everybody does," she said. "Any girl would want one. Wouldn't they, Alberta?"

"Some of them would," Alberta said helpfully.

"Well, wouldn't *you* want one?"

"Mother," Chevy said. "I've already asked Alberta to marry me, and she's already turned me down. There's no hope. Just turn off the high pressure, please." He offered his mother a smile which he hoped was appropriate for the moment, but he did not look at Alberta.

"You must have a guilty conscience, Chevy," his mother said slyly. "I was talking about *Daniel's* wedding, but you keep trying to change the subject and bring up *your* wedding." As she spoke one of her eyebrows rose higher than the other one in a look of great cunning.

"I'm sure glad you don't write the history books, Mom, we'd be in one hell of a . . ."

"But you did, Chevy," Alberta said, joining merrily in the family fun. "You brought it up."

"That's right!" Mrs. Callister said with a little shriek. "We women have to stick together."

Chevy's face changed. It was clear that he felt some special confidence had been violated. He mumbled something that couldn't be understood.

"You must let me show you my flowers, Alberta," his mother was saying. "Do you like flowers?"

"Sure."

"C'mon, Berta, you don't like flowers," Chevy said in a very threatening way.

"Sure I do. I think they're neat."

Chevy mumbled something again.

"What?" his mother said.

"I said private detectives aren't supposed to like flowers." It had the dark, thick sound of something that has been intensely brooded over.

"Private detective?" Mrs. Callister said, and even her husband looked up.

"I took a course once," Alberta explained, ". . . out of a magazine."

"She did everything but get the license," Chevy said coldly and deliberately, as if winning himself a great point by revealing this.

"What an interesting thing," Mrs. Callister said, full of admiration.

"You did?" said Mr. Callister with his largest smile of the afternoon.

"Well," Alberta said, becoming shy and wrinkling up her nose, "I was only a kid and I had some pretty dumb ideas."

"How wonderful," Mrs. Callister said, clapping her hands together.

Chevy had begun to blink very rapidly. His lips were slightly parted and his eyes were startled and blind-looking as if he had been searching for something in a dark room and the lights had just been switched on. He sat like that for several seconds while his mother cooed to Alberta.

"What do you hope to be?" Mr. Callister was asking.

"I don't want to *be*, I want to *do*," Alberta said, laying down her fork seriously in the manner of Mrs. Callister.

"Pardon me?" Mr. Callister said.

"No!" Alberta covered her eyes briefly with her hand. "I screwed it up," she explained. "I mean it's Chevy who wants to be, and I want to do *and* be, and you're the ones who do." She looked toward Chevy. "Right?" she asked hopefully.

Chevy did not look at her at all. "What she wants," he said, ". . . is to be an honest huckster with one of those traveling county fairs."

Mr. Callister laughed good-naturedly and looked toward his wife. "Now that's the kind of high ambition I'd expect from the kind of girl who could get Chevy to fly a kite in the Promenade on a windless day." The two of them laughed, and Chevy smiled, gripping his fork as if he might do violence with it.

"Oh, this is wonderful," Mrs. Callister said. "We're so glad you could come, Alberta. Sunday hasn't been so much fun in a long time. Isn't that right, Arnold?"

"Mmmmmm!" Arnold said. "Absolutely!"

"Yeah," Alberta said. "Boy, and to think we were gonna have bananas and some cold cheeseburgers that Beanie fixed last night."

"Beanie?" asked Mrs. Callister.

"Beanie is the fellow Alberta works for," Chevy said. "Alberta works fifty-four hours a week in a restaurant."

Mr. Callister stopped his fork an inch from his lips, and Mrs. Callister placed her fork beside her plate in alarm. "So *much!*" she said.

"She was working her way through college — for a while," Chevy said.

"Did you have any financial help other than your own salary?" Mr. Callister asked, his fork still poised.

"Beanie co-signed a note for me." She was embarrassed again, leaning over her plate.

"Not many girls do *that*," Mrs. Callister said. "Not even many boys do that."

"Eighteen percent of the boys, and less than one percent of the girls," Mr. Callister said, lowering the fork. "I made the survey myself."

"Maybe no percent of the girls now," Chevy said.

"But I don't want to go back anyway," Alberta said.

"Only sixteen percent of freshmen dropouts return to school again."

"Alberta isn't a dropout! She didn't *drop* out!"

Even Chevy was amazed and a little frightened by the pregnancy, the heaviness, the over-loaded portentousness of his few words. They hung threateningly in the air over the table and demanded to be examined. During the long silence while the words hung, three of the people at the table did not lift their eyes to see what the fourth now realized. There was only the sound of forks spearing through beef roast and touching china and the creak of uncomfortable bodies in wooden chairs. The chin of the fourth person had taken on the texture of a walnut shell, and it held this for several moments. Then suddenly Mrs. Callister leaned forward and made a flurry in the center of the table with her hands, rearranging bowls, attempting by sheer physical energy and presence to dispel the previous mood of the discussion.

"Well," said Mrs. Callister. "Here it is the Fourth of July."

The other three looked up attentively, as if hoping for even more information of equal weight and consequence.

"My my," continued Mrs. Callister, smiling pointedly around the room. "How time flies."

"Yes," said both her husband and son, nodding.

"Alberta," Mrs. Callister said, "I see you're through. Let's you and I get the men their coffee and then go out and see those flowers."

Alberta pushed her plate away and rose and the two women left. From the kitchen the two men heard chuckling and giggling, and after a few moments louder laughter. Then the voice of Mrs. Callister:

"This has just been more fun," she was saying. "If you don't come again, we'll be so disappointed." Then they heard Alberta affirm that yes, she would come again. She sure would.

LABOR DAY

THE RUB OF LOVE

If I were tickled by the rub of love,
A rooking girl who stole me for her side,
Broke through her straws, breaking my bandaged
string,
If the red tickle as the cattle calve
Still set to scratch a laughter from my lung,
I would not fear the apple nor the flood
Nor the bad blood of spring.

Dylan Thomas

It was absurd the way it happened. For supper last night Ellen had fixed pork chops, and she had fixed them dry and hard — the way she liked them. The pork chop thing was one of her just-because-I'm married-I-won't-be-deprived-of-my-personality gestures which she felt called upon to make once or twice a week. Not that Daniel minded, in fact he definitely approved. But on the other hand he had to gesture back.

"Marvelous!" he had said. "Terrific! Boiled owl. My favorite taste treat." There was no malice in his voice. Actually he was in genuine high spirits. If the truth were told, he was actually beginning to prefer his pork chops crisp. His error, he reflected, was in failing to take into account her mood.

Daniel had discovered that these were two moods. The normal mood — a little arch and defensive, obliquely humorous — was what he had come to call her Lauren Bacall mood. In the presence of this mood Daniel found himself as Bogart, and they would sometimes go on for hours this way. Her other mood, however, the one she had been in at supper, left him no complementary role. In this mood she played the Queen of Sheba — aloof, serene, caustic. As the Queen of Sheba she was entirely unapproachable, and he normally gave her regality silent respect or at most, light humor.

But she had failed to see the humor of the owl comment, and she replied with a cool, acid monologue which, for the first few minutes, sounded almost prepared before it skidded suddenly out of control.

Daniel had waited too long to reply. He knew that now. He had waited until he had been caught up in her emotion, and when he finally did strike back he struck too hard and too much into the nerve center of things.

There had been a second of silence after his words while they both gathered themselves.

"And what the hell is *that* supposed to mean?" she said.

"What the hell do you *think* it means?" He was already sorry, but it was too late.

"You can just tell me what you meant by that, please," she said. She was regal again, and controlled.

"What do you do?" he asked, his own voice deep in his throat sounding harsh and unfamiliar to his ears, ". . . spend all day figuring ways to turn me off? You're sick, you're tired, you've got a headache, you . . ."

"What am I supposed to do? Start panting because you roll over? You've got a few things to learn, *lover!*" She could do terrible things with a word when she wanted to.

"And what the hell is *that* supposed to mean?" Daniel said.

"If the shoe fits wear . . ."

"Just start explaining! That is, if you even know what you . . ."

"If the goddamned shoe . . ."

"Just start exp . . ."

"If you think you're the world's greatest lover, you've got another think *coming!*" She had lost her serenity by this time, and he was a little cowed by her violence. He turned back to his meal in disdain.

"You wouldn't know a good screw . . ." he began.

"Wouldn't I? *Wouldn't* I? Do you think I grew up in a monastery, *lover?*"

Daniel's lips curled for a response, but Ellen's flushed, almost eager expression froze the words in his throat. By the time his faculties returned any reply at all would have seemed thought out and considered. It was too late to slam out of the house, too late to hit her. Those first few seconds of quailed, overpowered speechlessness were left to stand finally and forever as his response. There was nothing to do but to pretend the whole thing was too specious to concern him, to feign a sarcastic laugh, to turn back and mechanically eat the meal and later to sit with an involved expression in front of the TV trying to think, trying to reason it all out, to fit this new fact into the fabric of their marriage. But there was Ellen, regal again and somehow frighteningly different. It had been very difficult to think.

And that night, lying on his side of the queen-sized

bed, he had been unable to sleep and he had been unable, yet, to think clearly about it. There were other distractions to blur and distort his thinking. Ellen, beside him, had begun breathing deeply and peacefully almost as soon as the lights were out, and after an hour Daniel realized in a quivering, sweating rage that she was not pretending to be asleep — she was, and it had been necessary, then, to conquer this incredible, biasing fact of her easy sleep. And when he had done this — cleared his mind of it — then the smaller things: the petty annoyances, the idiosyncrasies, the things about her that he had gritted his teeth against and tried to adjust himself to — these began a parade through his mind in a relentless series of brief vignettes: Ellen methodically separating the meat from the fat in the morning's bacon; Ellen casually sniffing yesterday's underpants to see if they would do service one more day; Ellen performing the incredible series of muscle-toning exercises and applying the endless beauty devices, creams and ointments; Ellen sugaring her frosted breakfast cereal.

But as he lay there Daniel fought them, steeling his mind and firming his will not to allow these things to color his considerations of the problem immediately at hand. He would, he assured himself, consider it and resolve it dispassionately and without prejudice.

But he could not think. It required all his mental energies simply to keep his judgment uninfluenced by the scenes that played ceaselessly through his mind — scenes which were now becoming more and more weighted in his favor and which put Ellen in an increasingly severe and unlovely light. He had to deal with these before he could think of the problem itself. Not that it was actually a problem, he reminded himself. What she had told him, or rather had hinted at — that wasn't the problem. The problem was that she was expecting something from him now, and he wasn't certain what it was. And even if he knew what she wanted, what she expected, he still didn't know what was *right*!

And the next morning other temptations presented themselves — other obstacles to be dealt with which stood before his consideration of the problem of what to do. The urge to leave the house without facing her was very great, but Daniel survived even that and forced himself to maintain the ritual that they had established. He had his two cups of coffee. He read the paper, commenting aloud on interesting items. But she said nothing. The yolks of his eggs were broken and his coffee was too weak. These were her only communications.

And during the morning at the office there was no work to do out of the office, no houses to show or see, none of the outdoors work that Daniel preferred. He sat hour after deadly hour in the monstrously comfortable, quiet, air-conditioned, carpeted and polished office holding his pencil to the unending flow of work which came to him from his mother's office. He could not think constructively about his own problems. There was no time. His only freedom from the work and from the eyes of the impossibly efficient, impossibly persevering Caroline McGregor, his mother's secretary, was the lavatory, and Daniel had already been there twice and it was not yet even noon. He had gone there both times to think, and had found himself not thinking, but instead watching his own face in the mirror. Not watching himself, exactly, or feeling sorry for himself, but only watching, as one watches in the dentist's waiting room an already too well-read magazine. And when he was back at his desk it seemed to him that his mind had been absolutely blank.

It was Saturday, and on Saturdays at Blake Realty they worked only half-days. There was no way for Daniel to avoid going home for lunch without obviously disrupting his normal pattern and showing that he was upset. No, he must go home, and before he did he must have resolved everything that needed to be resolved. Time was running out.

When only a few minutes remained before noon, Daniel left again for the lavatory. He did not stop in front of the mirror this time, but walked resolutely past it and into the single small stall. He lowered his pants, holding the belt buckle in his palm so that it would not jingle, and sat.

All right, he told himself. Time to think now. Something must be done to set things straight again. Something! Okay? And if anything was clear in this whole mess it was that whatever he did, it would have to be rather spectacularly different from anything he'd ever done before. She was expecting something from him — something big. The way she'd watched him last night and again this morning had told him that. She was waiting for something, and she was perfectly capable of waiting forever.

But why had she made such a big production out of it? Blown it all out of proportion? It made it so difficult to think clearly about it. Of course he'd been a little stunned at first. Who wouldn't be? But it was pretty clear, or it should be by now, that he wasn't affected as she had apparently expected. Now that he thought about it his reaction last night had been exactly right. Not say a word. Not show any emotion at all. Not even show any damned concern. If he'd done anything, argued or became angry, that would have shown that he was really bothered by it, and of course he was not!

Why couldn't she see that he didn't give a damn what she had done before he met her? What was he, some prude? So she wasn't a virgin. What did she expect him to feel? Deprived? Cheated?

As he sat there the bitterness rose in him again, and he began to wonder about the baby.

Daniel placed one hand over both his eyes as if trying to shut out all the light. He had tried before to think about this, and it was very painful. The pieces were all there and several times he had almost fitted them together, but somehow when he got too near a solution everything blurred and went out of focus. On the one hand it was difficult to believe that she had not been responsible — that she had not willfully and with forethought planned and executed the whole affair. But on the other hand it seemed impossible that Ellen would have or that she could have organized and carried out such a thing by herself. Now that it was over he had never found the courage to discuss it with her. He had never found the mood, really, in which it could be discussed. But she *must* have been responsible. There was too much evidence.

The night, for example, that he had found her in the

scalding tub, her body lobster red, her wrinkled, prune-like feet and hands showing how long she had been soaking. It had been necessary for him to help her out of the water and to bed. But she would not allow him to call a doctor. It was a beauty treatment she said, and Daniel, who had seen her also apply a little sandstone block to her elbows and knees, another beauty treatment, believed her.

And there were the picnics — the hiking which to his surprise she had begun to want to do nearly every weekend — which involved day-long drives to the mountains in the west. She would grimly climb in the July and then August sun until the sweat poured from her and until she was gasping for air. And Daniel thought that the climbing was for him, that she was attempting to make of herself an outdoors girl just for him.

But Daniel, pleased as he was about the hikes, had many times asked her to slow down, to stop and rest, to climb no farther or not to climb at all. At first he had just assumed that she knew better than he about such matters, but finally one day he had asked uncertainly if the strain might be hard on the baby.

As before when he had brought up the proposal of finding a name, she reacted as if the mention of it were an unspeakable affront to her delicacy — an act so low as not to warrant a reply at all.

And when they returned from the mountains she would spend great amounts of time locked alone in the bathroom. She was in the tub again, he could tell that, and once he had heard her vomit.

He should have known, it was true, just as he should have known when he opened the door once on the bedroom to find her sitting calmly on the edge of the bed with an ominously straightened coathanger. But she had not made any attempt to hide it. She had not acted the guilty, caught, potential self-aborter. She had smiled and reached with it over her shoulder, and she had calmly scratched her back.

It had occurred to him, of course, that Ellen was trying to lose the baby, but Daniel's first reaction upon finding this thought in his mind was to rebuke himself for having considered it. He reasoned that though she might have conceivably wanted to do such a thing, she would not do it without consulting him, the father; and if she did want to do it, she would certainly have solicited his help — help which he probably would have given.

But Daniel did not think farther than to make this self-recrimination, and after doing that, he put the matter in suspension, awaiting the remaining information on the matter, information which he felt certain would — which he hoped would — show him to have been in the wrong, and would show Ellen to be guiltless.

The place in his mind where he put suspended considerations such as these had been filling rapidly since his marriage. So many things had occurred which he was unable to understand, which resulted from this strange and unpredictable female psyche which seemed to have, after all, its own special unknown logical order and sequence.

At first Daniel had attempted to understand difficulties as he came to them, and to correct aberrations in her thinking and actions as soon as he understood them. But somehow he had not been allowed to do this. The same thing happened when he challenged her. He would patiently reduce her, step by logical step to the point where there was no alternative to her admitting that she was wrong or illogical or misinformed, but at that point she would simply refuse to go farther — refuse to take that final step. She would threaten to produce so much anger and wrath and indignation that the fact of her admission would be lost, and at this point Daniel himself would retreat, seeing that if he pushed for the final admission he would only be embroiling himself in something which might color his life for days. It was just not worth it.

And so Daniel was not eager to question. He had decided to wait until the whole pattern of how she thought and acted had become clear to him. He would wait until all the facts were in before he began drawing conclusions, before he judged her or attempted to change her.

That was why when she suggested that the two of them get totally drunk, and that they do it alone, together in the house, he was not suspicious. Ellen did not like to drink — she did not understand drinking — and he told himself that it was an attempt on her part to learn to share the things that he enjoyed. But she had gone about it all wrong, drinking grimly and joylessly and almost doggedly until she became so sick that she began to throw up, and continued to throw up for what seemed to Daniel, who was holding her head, a long while. About the time of the early morning that she became coherently sober, Ellen began to have pains, but she waited for a long time before she finally allowed Daniel to call the doctor.

When the doctor had gone and the miscarriage was over — his mother on one side of the queen-sized bed holding one of Ellen's hands and he on the other — Daniel had been unable, quite, to believe the look on Ellen's face.

And now, his belt buckle still clasped in his hand in the dark, green-painted well of the stall, Daniel could not quite rid his mind of that expression. It filled him with apprehension and even in memory it frightened him. And as with everything else it threatened to warp and distort any consideration of the problem which he must solve now. He attempted, by sheer force of will, to change the direction of his thought.

Okay! Okay! Okay! he told himself. What is the important thing? The important thing is to impress on Ellen that he knew what should and shouldn't be considered important. The pre-marital screwing around was *not* an important thing. It was *not!* He'd have to let her know how he felt about it. He'd have to let her know that he did not give a damn what she had done before he met her. That was *her* business. There was no reason for her to get upset about it. Or guilty either. That was very important. She should absolutely not feel guilty about it. They'd just sit down like mature, intelligent adults and discuss it.

Daniel's hand was still pressed over his eyes, and under it his mouth was slightly open in an odd and strange way, as if he were having difficulty breathing.

Okay! he thought. The only thing left to decide is how to do this most effectively. How to let her know. How to initiate the discussion.

He removed the hand from across his eyes.

But dammit! She had no right to have made such a

scene about it — to have forced him into this position. Especially when she was the one who'd made all the pretensions to purity.

How many, Daniel wondered. One? Ten? Twenty? Not, of course, that it made any difference, but the idea of the deception — that she had consciously used time and energy trying to put him on about it —that was what mattered. Any change in the way he felt about her, and there was, dammit, there was a change — there couldn't help but be — this change was made by the knowledge that she was the kind of person who'd deceive and lie.

But Goddammit, why didn't she know that he hadn't expected to find her wrapped in cellophane. This was the twentieth century, and he'd been born after the Second World War, for *Christ's sake!* How could she have believed that it mattered? And if she thought that it was so damned wrong, then *why the hell did she do it?* And even if she did it, then why did she have to talk about it? Why did she have to use it as a weapon?

Daniel took a deep breath and pressed his hand even more firmly to his eyes. His job now was to convince her that as a weapon it was absolutely unlethal, absolutely harmless. He was proof against it. Okay then. He'd just let her know — make her *see* — that it wasn't important. Show her! What was important was what they were at the moment, not what they had been or had done in the past. Their concern should be with each other. The past was their private property. He didn't care about it. He didn't even want to know about it. The one or ten or twenty men in her past were her business entirely, okay?

He took another deep breath and lifted himself from

the commode and left the cubicle and stood outside the door. He zipped and buckled and retucked his shirt. He stood there for a long moment, his mouth open again awkwardly. Then, without his having known or planned, he put his fist through the pasteboard wall just above the urinal.

II

"What happened to the hand?" Ellen asked as he walked in. Her voice was caught somewhere between surprise and nonchalance.

"Had a flat and slammed the trunk lid on it. Few scratches." He strode toward her and took her in his arms and kissed her hard, then left her standing there while he threw himself into the big chair opposite the TV. "What's for lunch?" he said. He was smiling his best smile.

She stood where he left her, unwilling to accept his mood, searching in it for insincerity.

He smiled some more. "Something smells pretty damn good."

Her face collapsed abruptly and she ran to where he was sitting and threw herself into his lap. "Oh, Daniel, I'm sorry," she said. "Oh, I'm so sorry." She began to cry, and he held her.

"Don't be sorry," Daniel said. "You mustn't be sorry." With the tips of his fingers he lifted her chin so that she could see his smile. "There's absolutely nothing to feel sorry about." He began to talk like Bogart. "Look, baby, let's assume you had a bad day. Okay! Huh?"

She dropped her eyes and spoke in her own voice, signaling to him just how important this was to her. "No!" she said. "Really, Daniel. It was a terrible thing to say. A wrong thing to say, and I'm sorry. I am!" Her eyes lifted and caught his and would not release them.

Daniel was shaken by the force of her sincerity and by her stricken face. He continued as Bogart. "Oh," he said, "you could have been a little more pleasant maybe . . ."

"Really!" she said. "Please, Daniel . . ."

His eyes fled to his thumb which now played under her ear, and he tried to match her earnestness with his own. "Yeah, I know. I'm pretty grouchy too. I know what you mean. I mean, I get mad too easy too, honey, and I say things I don't mean . . ."

She pushed his hand away from her hair and stiffened in his lap. "Daniel," she said. "I'm trying to talk about . . ."

"I know you are," he said, "but I don't want to talk about it that way. You see, I don't care about that. Not at all. Not a damn bit."

He reflected over his words and he was pleased at his own dispassionateness, and his firmness and resolution.

"You don't care, huh?" She slowly stood. "You don't care, huh?"

On the second repetition her voice and face broke and she turned, running toward the bedroom. He heard her turn the lock just as he got to the door.

"Hey, Ellen?" He was bewildered. "What's the matter? Hey!"

"How can you . . . how . . . how can you be so ca . . .

ca . . . callous?" sobbed the voice on the other side of the door.

"What . . ." he said. "What . . ."

"How can you . . . You *bastard!*" she shrieked.

Then it happened again. His body rocked back and his bandaged hand leaped out to sink into the hollow plyboard door; then, in perfect rhythm, he rocked again and his foot hit just beside the knob, splintering the door inward. Ellen backed away, her hands over her mouth, her eyes bright and wide. Daniel's hand flew out again and Ellen spun sideways toward the bed. "You *whore!*" he screamed.

He was almost to the front door when she caught him.

"Don't go!" she cried. "Oh, please don . . . don't go!" Both her arms were locked around his waist and her body hung limp to the floor — her face in the small of his back. "I'm sorry," she said. "I didn't know that you felt that . . . that way! Don't go! Please don't go!" Her voice trailed off in a series of pleases.

Then, abruptly, the moment was gone for him, and as his mind cleared she led him the several steps back into the living room, across the new rug, where she fell with him on the new couch.

"Oh, my God!" He touched her face with frightened fingers. "Oh, I'm sorry," he said. "I didn't know . . ."

"No!" she said, flat against him, burrowing. "It's *me.* It's *my* fault, mine!!"

He held up his hand, hating it, glad for the pain. "Oh, Ellen! Really! I didn't want this to happen. I can't . . . oh God . . . I can't believe it did. I don't know . . ."

"You had every right. It was a ter . . . terrible thing I said to you." She was sobbing uncontrollably. ". . . a terrible thing."

"I'd give anything if it hadn't happened." He held her to him with his left arm, his eyes tight, his right hand held awkwardly in the air, the blood in long lines nearly to the elbow.

"I love you," she said. "You must believe that I've never loved anybody but you."

"Everything was so perfect — so straight in my mind. I can't understand how it happened. I wanted to . . ."

"Please forgive me!" She lifted her head to look at him for a second, then she dropped it again to his chest. "Please," she pleaded. "Please tell me how I can make it up to you. Tell me . . ."

"God*damn* it!" he said. "Why did it have to happen. I don't understand . . ."

"I was *young!* I didn't know . . ." Her voice was a wail of anguish.

"How could I have been so stupid?" he said, looking at the hand. "Blind! Blind! Blind!"

"Can you ever . . . will you ever be able to . . . to love me again?" She was quiet on his body, her hot cheek to his, her tears tracing an itchy path past his ear. "I'll do anything!" she said. ". . . anything."

He tried to make her sit up, to look at him, but she clung close in fear. "How can I . . ." he said. "You've got to let me . . ."

"I want to save the mar . . . marriage." Her body began to heave convulsively.

"Yes," he said. "Yes, yes, yes." He lifted her again by the shoulders, this time successfully, and made her face him. "Listen," he said. "This has been . . . this has been one of the most terrible things that's ever happened to me. I can't even . . . I . . ."

She tried to throw herself against him again with a fresh outbreak of anguish.

"How could I have done it?" she said. "I don't know how I . . ."

"No!" he said. "Listen, please. You've got to forgive me. If you can do that I . . . I promise that it will never happen again." His throat began to close and tears filled the corners of his eyes.

She began to look alarmed. "No!" she said. "No, Daniel. It's *me.* I . . ."

"Please," he said. "Please. I don't know how it happened. Nerves! Nerves! I've been awfully nervous." He took a deep breath, trying to stop his tears. "I've been having — Oh, Ellen, I've been having an awful time at the office. I hate it! I can't stand it! And then we had that stupid fight. I don't know what got into . . ."

She slid slowly from the couch and began to back away from him, her face lopsided with the scarlet swelling under one eye.

"You son-of-a-bitch," she said softly. "You son-of-a-bitch."

And for the second time in twenty-four hours his mind numbed before her. He could only watch as she whirled and walked into the bedroom. He could hear a chair being moved against the broken door.

He sat rigidly where she had left him for several minutes until the throbbing in his hand drove him up and to the bathroom to search for Mercurochrome and bandages. The hand was suddenly quite painful, but the bleeding had stopped of its own accord by the time he discovered that he could not cut, wrap and tape with only one good hand. He sat on the lidded commode.

How the hell did all this get started? he asked himself. She was just not acting rationally at all. There was something here that just defied logic.

But there had really not been enough time to think. The whole day had just been impossible so far. Not enough sleep last night. Maybe later this afternoon he could try again.

He left the bathroom and wandered for a moment, glancing occasionally at the quiet broken bedroom door. Then he flicked on the TV and sat in the big chair, a troubled frown on his face.

III

In the morning, after Ellen had taken all the aspirin, she returned to the bathroom and stood for several moments in front of the mirror. The swelling had gone down and had left a reddish, purple mark which spread from the tip of the cheekbone — growing pinker — to the edge of the eye. She lifted her fingertips now and drew them softly around the edge of the mark several times in a polishing motion. Her eyes locked on the eyes in the mirror as if searching for something there, for a reaction or a sign.

But Ellen found no pain there or grief, but only . . . what? Sorrow? she asked herself. Regret?

Yes, regret, she decided. Regret and pity! Not for herself but for Daniel — good, good Daniel who would be blamed and who would suffer. Yes, he loved her — foolish, good Daniel, Ellen thought, and for that he had suffered and must suffer more. Those who found her body would not know that the bruise and all that had happened yesterday — that these were not responsible for what she had done. They would not know.

Ellen saw now in her mind the officers who would be called. They lifted back the sheet and they saw the bruised eye and they looked meaningfully at each other. They called another man, a man in white, a doctor who began to examine her further.

Ellen widened her eyes at herself in the mirror. She hadn't thought of that. She moved quickly to the bedroom where she laid out fresh underthings and began to disrobe. But when she was naked and in front of the long, full-length mirror, Ellen noticed another bruise on the outside of her left thigh where the car door had blown shut on her. It wasn't dark or angry-looking, and even pressing on it there was no pain. But Ellen began to wonder what the doctor and the officers would think when they saw it. What would they say to Daniel about it? Would they accuse him of that too? She pictured Daniel's rage, his grief, perhaps striking out at the officers, and she was overcome by compassion. She hoped that Daniel would be brave.

"Be brave, Daniel," she whispered aloud. "Oh, be brave!"

Perhaps it would be necessary after all to leave a note. Perhaps it would be necessary to explain that Daniel was not responsible for the bruise on the leg — that he was not responsible for what she had done.

But no! She had determined not to leave a note. Notes were melodramatic and dishonest. Notes were written by people who were after sympathy or pity — by people who wished to blame someone else — who were unwilling, really, to cut off all ties with the world. No! No! This thing that she was doing was to be a private thing, an entirely personal thing. It was to be the one entirely honest and unselfish act of her life. It would be so honest and unselfish that she would even forgo the pleasure of informing others of its honesty and selflessness.

She realized that she had better dress herself. How long had it been since she had taken the aspirin? Less than five minutes, and there was nothing yet — no reaction.

In the clean panties and bra she turned sideways to the mirror, and her eyes traveled up the gentle line from the thighs to the breasts. She tightened the muscles, making the line flat, and then relaxed herself. There was still a small, more than supple, unwanted roundness of the under belly remaining from the pregnancy. Another few weeks and it would have been entirely gone. She almost regretted that she couldn't wait until it was the same as it had been before. But no! Ellen snuffed out this thought.

Then, thinking of this, Ellen realized something else. Wouldn't the examination reveal that she had been pregnant and that she had miscarried? Wouldn't that be in the papers too with the story of her death, and wouldn't Daniel be thought responsible for that too? The possibility drove her back to the bathroom where she offered a frightened look to herself in the mirror.

"Will they know?" she asked in a whisper. "Will they know?"

Ellen knew now that she would have to leave a note. She would do it for Daniel. For him she would deprive herself of the last and most sacred dignity and honesty left to her — a quiet and murmurless death. For Daniel she would go through the agony of revealing everything, taking all the blame on herself. He must suffer no more for having loved her.

Ellen, thinking of Daniel, shed her first tears of the morning, brushing them gently from her bruised eye. Earlier she had not cried when she was wakened by the sound of Daniel leaving the couch in the living room where he had slept, and she hadn't cried a moment later when he was gone, shutting the door quietly behind him. Even as the car in the driveway started and her husband drove away from her — even then Ellen did not cry. It had seemed to her that she was beyond tears. She had been awake only moments. The shades were still drawn and her eyes were still closed against the new day, and Ellen had already recognized and accepted that this would be the most terrible and crushing day of her ill-starred and blighted life. Today, she knew, would deliver the final, annihilating blow. And why? Why was it that the unwavering purpose — high purpose — and the diligent application of will and intellect — why had they all come to only this? Why, she asked herself, did everything happen to her?

On the queen-sized bed Ellen dreamed for a moment, as she often did in trying times, of an all-seeing, all-just, heavenly tribunal who were keeping and had kept an unflagging record of the injuries done to her, and of the slights cast in her face by an insensitive and hard world. She dreamed that alongside these slings and arrows was also a balance sheet of the equanimity and understanding and patience with which she had met these slights and injustices — a careful and exact record.

But this morning the tribunal did not report as it always had. There was a new and unexpected element, a new member who insisted that another version of the history be shown, who brought forward new evidence. And once he began, the new member turned over every stone in the foundation of her life, challenging every motive and showing it to have been characterized by greed and pretension and dishonesty. Once he was started he could not be stopped, and within minutes her life, her blamelessly organized and executed life was revealed with unmistakable clarity to be an incredible patchwork of selfishness and artificiality.

Ellen had lain paralyzed under the weight and impact and the suddenness of it, thinking, knowing that there was but one thing of honesty left for her which, if it would not annul and correct the past, would at least put an end to the pattern of error and wrong which characterized her life. Ellen knew that there could be, for her, no future.

But even then she had not cried. The knowledge, terrible as it was, had strengthened her, calmed her remarkably and cleared her vision. For the next several minutes she examined this evidence again, and again she pronounced judgment upon herself. She had no further need of rationalizations or defenses. Objectivity comes easy for those with but hours to live.

It had been with a calmness, then, and with detachment that Ellen rose from the bed. Daniel had no guns, and she had never known a need for sleeping pills, but in the medicine cabinet there was a large, nearly empty, economy-sized bottle of aspirin, and beside it, a smaller bottle half full. Ellen began to swallow the tablets one by one with water, but soon she began to fill up with liquid, and some of the tablets began to feel as if they were lodged in her throat and it became necessary to drink even more water to wash these down. Ellen looked at the amount of tablets left and moved to the kitchen where she began to crush them on the bread board with the handle of a knife. When she had finished she put the powder into a glass of tomato juice. It did not mix well. At first it floated in a little white mound, and even after she had stirred it vigorously with a fork the juice looked lumpy and unpleasant. But Ellen was able to drink it, her eyes closed and one hand at her throat.

That was five minutes ago, and Ellen was now wondering if her breath was coming faster, more labored. She felt for her pulse, but couldn't find it. There was still a sticky, lumpy sensation in the back of her throat, a feeling that some of the aspirin were still lodged there. Ellen went again to the kitchen to try to wash them down with more tomato juice, but the feeling would not go away. She began to wonder if they would pump her stomach even after she was dead to find out how many pills she had taken, and at the thought of this her stomach began to churn wildly. Perhaps she should leave the note after all. This would be another thing necessary to tell.

But whatever the purity of her motive, wouldn't her explanations, her careful remarks about the bruises, the pill-counting, wouldn't this seem like so much melodrama?

She couldn't leave a note, and she couldn't *not* leave one.

Ellen began to be frightened — not of her impending doom, but that even this last act as everything else would be awkwardly and imperfectly done, that it would be characterized after all by artificialities and selfishness. And worst of all (why hadn't she thought of this before?), what if her death appeared to be nothing more than a mere accident and not a work of her will and self-determination after all?

During the next two minutes Ellen began several notes, writing hurriedly at the kitchen table on small pieces of paper torn from the shopping list pad. But when she was finished she realized that she must dispose of the uncompleted and abandoned beginnings of notes — there were several — or it would be clear to whoever found her that she had worried about careful wording and composition, and that too would certainly, and rightly, be seen as more artificiality, more phoniness.

It took Ellen several minutes to flush them, one by one, down the toilet, and at the last minute she flushed also the completed final draft and then stood in front of the mirror and began, for the second time, to cry. She found herself speaking to the mirror, speaking with agonizing sincerity, spilling forth all the things that needed to be expressed. The explanations behind the explanations on the note — everything. Then, almost violently, she whirled herself away from the mirror and covered her face with her hands. She couldn't talk to a mirror! What she really needed was a person, a friend to talk to.

She glanced at her watch. Ten minutes had elapsed since taking the pills. She did not know how much time was left. She felt for her pulse as she walked toward the phone but again she could not find it. But in the yellow pages of the phone book she immediately found the name of the restaurant and she called Alberta Raynes.

As she waited for Alberta to answer, Ellen did not even consider what she might say or what might be said to her when the voice appeared on the other end. She only knew that her time was running out and that she must act on impulse — act on the information which was flowing now out of that vast storehouse of the subconscious — information which told her that the only other truly honest person, the only living person who might possibly offer a sympathetic and patient ear, who would know and recognize sincerity and honesty, would be Alberta Raynes. Since that night at the party Alberta had stayed strangely in her mind, had resided uncomfortably in its dark corners like an unsolved problem or like something waiting to be remembered. Although Ellen had not met her again, she had discovered many things about her from Daniel and had once stood for several minutes outside the aluminum door of the restaurant where Alberta worked, nearly going in for coffee and conversation.

"Hello?" It was unmistakably the voice of Alberta Raynes.

"Alberta? Miss Raynes? This is Ellen Curry — I mean Ellen Blake." Now why had she done that? She hadn't done that in months! "We met at my wedding party a couple of months ago."

"Yes?" There was nothing antagonistic in the girl's voice.

"Well, I . . . I have a favor to ask of you. I'm sorry, I know I don't have a right to ask you for anything, but I really must." Ellen had been trying to keep the tension and panic from her voice, but it had come out all wrong in a languid, almost bored tone. "I mean it's rather an emergency. I really have to." Ellen now let her voice go where it would, hoping only that it would sound genuine.

"Oh? What can I do for you?" Still not antagonistic or annoyed. Not anything. Wary, perhaps.

"Could you come over? To my house, I mean? Right now? It's your day off, isn't it?"

"Yes," Alberta said after a moment.

"Could you? Please? It's . . . it's the most important thing . . ." Ellen paused, biting her lip, ". . . of my life."

"What's the address?"

Ellen gave it to her. "Please hurry," she said. "Oh, please!" and she hung up.

After Ellen left the phone she began to pace the living room, speaking aloud and gesturing, reviewing in her mind the things she would say to Alberta, the confessions that she would make, the honest things about herself that she would finally make known, the truths she would tell. She would first ask Alberta not to interfere, not to call a doctor or an ambulance, and she would tell her about how the bruise on the leg was an accident, and about the miscarriage, and about how many pills.

But wouldn't that incriminate the girl? When the doctors and the officers and Daniel found out that Alberta had been here, that she had talked to Ellen and hadn't done anything to prevent her from taking her own life, wouldn't Alberta then be held responsible?

Oh, God, Ellen moaned, she had made a mess of it after all. Such a simple thing, and she had done it all wrong. She closed her eyes tightly and compressed her lips and tried not to cry for a third time. She tried to think what to do.

But now her stomach felt bad, and suddenly . . . yes, there was a throbbing in her temples. Ellen concentrated on the throbbing, trying to measure its exact intensity. Was death by aspirin overdosage painful? She hadn't thought of that at all. She glanced at her watch. Oh, God, it was ten minutes since she'd called. Perhaps Alberta wouldn't get here in time.

"Oh, hurry," Ellen whispered. "Hurry!"

If she could just die while Alberta was here. That would solve all the problems. She concentrated on the throbbing. Was it worse?

But what if Alberta didn't believe her? What if she didn't believe that Ellen had taken the aspirin at all? Then suddenly she knew how to solve all the problems. She would convince Alberta that it was too late to call.

She went to the kitchen and got the two aspirin bottles. She returned to the living room and laid the bottles on the rug and then she lay down beside them.

Then the doorbell rang.

Ellen continued to lie there, and after several rings she heard the door open slowly and cautiously and after a moment she knew someone was in the room with her, moving on the rug. Ellen lay still, waiting for a hand to touch her shoulder or her forehead, waiting for arms to tug her to her feet and try to walk her. Had this happened, Ellen would have known exactly what to do, but this did not happen, and after several seconds when no helping and sympathetic hands had reached to help her Ellen began to be frightened. Who could it be? It couldn't be Alberta or Daniel. Perhaps it was a neighbor or a delivery man. But no, either of these would have tried to get her up or would have run shouting for help or called someone on the telephone. It must be, oh God, a *burglar*.

The burglar moved quietly behind her, and, the sound was unmistakable, sat on the couch and opened a magazine.

Ellen tried to control her breathing, pretending to be unconscious. Why doesn't he take what he wants and leave? she asked herself. Is he waiting for a helper? Ellen pictured a truck parking in front of the door and the thieves — she'd read about such things — the thieves taking every stick of furniture in the house. She could see them stepping carefully over her body.

And wouldn't the officers then think that she had been murdered? That she had been forced to eat the aspirin by the thieves? And what of Alberta? While behind her the thief was turning the pages of the magazine one by one, Ellen planned that when Alberta came in she would leap to her feet and scream a warning. Yes. It was the only fair thing to do.

Then behind her the burglar left the couch and Ellen could tell that he was walking around to the front of her. She opened one of her eyes a slit, and near her head she saw not burglar's shoes, not even a man's shoes, but instead the unmistakable, thick, red soles of Alberta's waitress shoes. Then Alberta knelt beside her, and Ellen heard the aspirin bottles picked up and clinked together and then dropped.

What was wrong? Ellen wondered. Did Alberta think she was already dead? Then why hadn't she felt her pulse? Had she already summoned doctors or the police and was she now just waiting? Ellen prepared a soft, mumbled moan such as drugged people might make — *live* drugged people, and she uttered it as the shoes departed from her.

Apparently Alberta did not hear. She was shutting and opening the broken bedroom door. She did this several times, and then Ellen heard her footsteps in the kitchen. She heard drawers opening — drawer after drawer. Then there was the sound of knives and forks, yes, it was unmistakable, and the opening of the aluminum bread box.

Ellen moaned again, louder, and altered her body position to one more comfortable. Certainly Alberta must now know that she was alive. She had seen the aspirin bottle and she must know what had happened. What was wrong?

Ellen heard walking on the rug and the sounds of chewing and swallowing seemed to echo in the silent room. From Ellen's new position she could see all of the girl. Alberta had made herself a peanut butter and jelly sandwich.

Ellen saw now that the girl didn't believe she was dying, didn't believe that she was unconscious. That *bitch*, that *chippy* thought that — that she was only *pretending* to be unconscious!

Ellen, lying on the new rug beside the two aspirin bottles in her clean underthings, began to blush, and she wished, wished, wished that she would die, really die. She *was* pretending to be unconscious. She knew she wouldn't die. She *was* pretending!

Across the room Alberta flicked on the television and sat in the big chair and began to watch a parade somewhere. It was Labor Day.

The parade continued for what seemed like hours during which Ellen noticed that the throbbing in her temples was diminishing and being replaced by a roiling and nausea in her stomach.

Then abruptly the TV was shut off and Alberta was kneeling down beside her, bending down and whispering. "Thanks for the sandwich," she said. "I won't say anything about this to anyone if you'll promise next time to use something besides aspirin, okay?"

Then she was gone.

Ellen continued to lie there for several minutes after she heard the front door close, her will to move and her powers of reflection completely paralyzed by shame. Then finally she scrambled to her feet and dashed into the bathroom where she threw up into the commode. After this she turned again to the mirror and stared critically for several minutes. Finally she spoke, not in a whisper but in a strong and stern and commanding voice.

"You through now?" Ellen asked. "You finished finally? You done about everything you can do?"

There was no answer from the mirror although Ellen waited for several moments, and then she left and made the bed and cleaned up the jam and peanut butter in the kitchen. While she was doing this, washing the knife and screwing the lid on the peanut butter jar, she began to laugh, and she laughed harder than she had in years.

That night Daniel, chiseling insets and planing the edge of the new door with his new plane, couldn't believe the way his wife was acting, couldn't believe the coffee she was bringing him and the attention she was lavishing on him. Could it be after all, he thought to himself, that they like to be belted around?

OVER THE FENCE

The rodeo had begun late in the afternoon, and now the sun had gone down and a slight fall chill had settled on the stands where Chevy sat with Alberta. Although Chevy was cold, he did not allow himself to shiver. He had made up his mind that he would like the rodeo at any cost. He would provide for Alberta a perfect day, not only because he was her guest, but because tonight he would tell her, finally, of his plans.

And so Chevy had shouted his way through the initial events, applauding and laughing and drinking beer bought in paper cups from the hawkers. With the calf roping, however, he had found himself talking in genuine excitement about the precision of horse and rider, the wordless, skilled, automatic coordination of the animal and the man. Alberta agreed politely to this, but she herself seemed unimpressed. Wait, she told him, for the bareback broncs.

And then came the bulldoggers, and when Chevy marveled at the courage of the men who leaped from their horses onto the necks and horns of galloping steers Alberta was only patronizing. Chevy was excited by the Brahma bulls, but this too was passed off by Alberta as unworthy. Once a rider was thrown heavily and did not rise. The crowd had come to its feet with an intake of breath, the only sound in the floodlit arena the hoarse pants and clanging neck-bell of the spinning Brahma. Then, just as he was noticed by the bull, the rider got to his feet and hobbled to the fence where he was lifted over. Chevy saw that Alberta had not risen with the crowd but had remained seated with her eyes tightly closed. He knew that she was thinking of her brother. And Chevy half expected to hear over the loudspeaker that Billy-the-Kid Raynes would be next out of chute number four on a Brahma bull named Blue-Tick. He was even a little disappointed when it did not happen.

It was with the saddle-bronc riding that Alberta began to come alive, pointing out special features to watch for in the rider — foot position high on the neck and free arm high. She schooled Chevy in techniques and sequences of bucking which signaled excellence in the horse. The rides, she explained, were terminated after eight seconds, and the eight seconds were judged on the combined qualities of horse and rider. The only real difference between saddle-bronc and bareback was that in the bareback the man had only a rope around the horse's middle to hold with one hand. For Alberta, the rest of the rodeo was mere window dressing for the broncs.

And there did seem to be a new element in the air when

the bareback events began. Chevy noticed that even the other riders lined the fence as spectators, and after the first ride there was a change of atmosphere in the stands. The shuffling discourtesy, the shouting and indiscriminately applauding spirit of the other events tensed into a quiet. Before each ride a charged silence entered the stands, and even up in the farthest seats the creak of the rope hinge could be heard as the gate opened, and the combined gasp of both horse and rope-connected man was audible as the two spun from the pen and into the arena for their eight-second mating. Man sounds and horse sounds — deep, from the belly and lungs — and now and again the pound of hooves as the horse touched briefly to the earth, rose clearly to the silent stadium. And there was none of the pure bravado of the Brahmas, no possibility of blood to account for this attention from the stands — this raptness. There was none of the polished grace of the calf roping — not strength only as with the dogging of the steers, but something else that touched unexpectedly deep and sure inside Chevy — a recognition, somehow, of what was happening there under the lights. He felt himself and all those in the stands merged with horse and rider in eight seconds of some higher, privileged purity which at other times — rare, rare and short-lived times — he had found with women or with men, rare moments when some balance was struck and held momentarily between equals before the balance was realized and understood away.

But in the arena there was no time for understanding, and the balance struck — held — extended for an infinity of eight seconds.

"Your brother does *this?*" Chevy said. ". . . all the time?"

Alberta smiled but she did not turn to him. "In the magazine thing," she said, ". . . you remember? They asked him how come he kept on riding and getting his legs broke all the time, and he said that he was waiting for some time when he could finish his eight seconds and then go over the fence, not bucking any more, but just going. You know?" She turned then and skipped her eyes once across his face without really stopping there, and then looked back into the arena. The next ride was ready to start.

"Uh-huh," Chevy said. "I know."

They said nothing else until it was over.

There was still some of the intoxication and spirit and breathlessness left unexpended in them when they spilled from the stands and out into the carnival area, and they could not laugh, talk, move or see fast enough. On the giant ferris wheel Alberta rocked the chair wildly at the top, and Chevy, white, did not protest. They drove Dodge-em cars, two adults in a wild traffic jam of children, laughing too hard to steer. Chevy threw balls first at leaden milk bottles and then at heavy-bottomed dolls. They shot at moving ducks, Alberta hitting two to Chevy's one and winning a button which said KISS ME QUICK! I'M DYING! Chevy strutted to the basketball toss, a former high school hero of the sport, and missed four of his first five shots. He was persuaded to swing the massive wooden mallet, sending the metal car up the runner past the words "Pantywaist!" "Creampuff!" "Mighty Mouse!" "Okay!" and nearly up to "Wow!" but not high enough to ring the bell and win the cigar. But at the dart throw he was a success, winning a huge black and white panda with celluloid button eyes and a pink ribbon around its neck by exploding six balloons in a row.

And when the carnival area could offer nothing more they visited the cereal produce display, and from there toured three long sweet-smelling barns where Alberta whispered to and touched the muzzle of the Grand Champion baby beef whose belly sagged into the deep carpet of straw. They examined the home-canned fruit and preserves, and at the fine arts hall Alberta smelled the winning flower displays and arrangements, coming away with pollen on her nose which Chevy started to brush away and then left.

And then at the exit of the last pavilion they could not avoid stopping to watch a fat man speaking urgently to a circle of listeners. He stood on a little platform at the back of a trailer-camper which folded down to reveal shelves of merchandise: cameras, watches, jewelry. A powerful light shone down from a stand on top of the camper, and it enclosed the group in a cone of light — at its center the fat man speaking, speaking, speaking. Chevy and Alberta stood a long time outside the circle of light, and when they finally left, it was wordlessly, Alberta hugging the panda to her chest with both arms and Chevy, hands in pockets, watching his feet walk.

In the car, the carnival noises and the enervating hum of the diesel motors shut out, they both realized that they did not want to be alone together. The radio helped to fill the silence, and they managed to say a few words about the evening, the rodeo and the fair, but the words were forced and the responses preoccupied. Chevy drove toward Beanie's to avoid the solitude and vastness of the church, and Alberta did not question his decision to do this.

But Beanie's too was empty. He had dismissed even the part-time girl. When Chevy and Alberta entered he poked his head briefly out of the kitchen door, his reading glasses far down on his nose, and then retreated, grumbling.

In the booth where they sat there was silence. Chevy flipped the selector leaves on the juke box while Alberta examined, stitch by stitch, her bear — both of them waiting for Chevy to begin speaking of the thing which was now expected.

But it was not to have been this way, and Chevy waited, desperately hoping for something to happen which would change the mood and the tone. It was to have been brought up in the afterglow of the rodeo and the carnival as a surprise, a bonus, a cause for added celebration. He had expected that there would be an easy, comfortable access to it. He had not expected that she would anticipate him or that she would have something of her own to tell.

"Well," he said abruptly, turning from the leaves, smiling, still uncertain what he would say next. ". . . well, now," he said. "Whilst you have been mindlessly living for the moment, thou careless grasshopper, the old ant here has been salting away goodies for the winter."

Alberta smiled at him. She took the bear and began to dance it on the table top. "Oh?" she said.

"Long, cold winter a-comin'," he said, "and you grasshoppers are gonna freeze your asses off."

She grinned, letting her eyes meet his for a second, but she did not stop dancing the bear, and she did not ask what.

"The old ant, howsomever, will be warm and cozy and full-bellied because he has made preparation."

"Preparation?" Alberta asked, interested, but not too interested, dancing still with the bear.

"He has procured for himself the best of all possible situations. He has arranged for himself to be in a place where there are many intellectually stimulating ant-happenings. And together with this also he will be paid to be in this place, and furthermore and alongside and in addition to this he will be doing a thing he enjoys doing, and he will be laying away ant-goodies for the winters to come."

The dancing bear stopped and she gave him her full attention. "Where?" she asked.

"Ann Arbor, Michigan," he said. It did not ring as full and solid and significant as he had hoped it would.

"Really?" she said. "What's there?"

"University of Michigan and one of the best graduate departments in the country for my field."

"No kidding?" Alberta said with a pleased slant of the head. "What? They offer you an assistantship there?"

He had wanted to say the words himself. "Yeah," he said. "That's right."

"That's great, Chevy."

"Pretty good news, huh?"

"Hey, it's neat."

"Pretty lucky, I guess."

"Lucky hell . . ." She reached across the table to bat his arm lightly.

"Aww . . ." Chevy said.

And they both continued to talk across the table to each other enthusiastically, both helping to fill all the blank spaces, two players in a long verbal volley. It was a way they had never talked before, and they seemed unable to stop it. Then finally Alberta asked the wrong question.

"Well," she said, "when did you find out about it? I mean, gee, it's almost time for school to start, and I thought you had to apply for those things really early in the year."

"Well actually, I applied last March," Chevy said immediately. "Just for the hell of it, you know. And I'm damned if they didn't offer me one." He began to play with the selector leaves again. "Well, at the time I didn't say yes and I didn't say no. Just kind of shelved the thing in case nothing better came along."

This too was the wrong thing to have said, and they both meditated on this fact during the silence that followed. Chevy took several toothpicks from the holder and began to break them. Alberta shook the bear, making the button eyes jump in their celluloid containers.

"Well, actually," he said after a moment, able to look at her only because she was not looking at him, "actually I weighed everything pretty carefully, and it will be the best thing for me to go ahead and get the Master's degree at least, you know?"

"Sure," Alberta agreed. "Do you think you might go

all the way and get a Ph.D. maybe? Do you think you might?"

"I don't know. Play it loose. Wait and see."

"You'll do very well, Chevy," she said, looking at him over the bear seriously. "You've got a good mind for that kind of thing."

"What kind of thing?" he asked, uncertain how this was meant, searching in it.

"School kind of thing," she said. "You'll get all A's and everything. Be the golden-haired boy and everything."

"It'll pass the winter," he said. "Us ants think about stuff like that. What're you grasshoppers gonna do?"

He had no sooner asked the question than he knew he did not want to hear the answer to it. He interrupted her before she could begin to speak.

"Freeze your asses off is what you're gonna do," he said. "Tell you what. I'm gonna save you the humiliation of having to come begging around come the first bad frost, and so I'll just come right out and invite you to avail yourself of my planning and forethought and all that. Can't stand to see a grasshopper shiver." He was pleased with the way he had done this, but though she smiled her appreciation, she shook her head.

"Aw, I don't think so, Chevy."

"Full belly," he said. "Warm bottom. Fringe benefits wall to wall."

She had only started to shake her head when he interrupted again.

"Don't you wanna hear about the fringies? Unbeatable. Hours? Hardly any at all. Half-time job at some plush

Dean's office winding electric clocks and such. Educational benefits? Free education in any department on campus. The horse department is, I understand, very fine there. Top-notch men in the field. Social benefits? Introduction to . . ."

"I really don't think so, Chevy." She tried to smile.

"Look, Berta, hell, we'd be living high. Four or five hundred a month between us. Really! You can't beat it! What's wrong?" He noticed that his hands were tightly closed, and he was leaning too intently forward. He relaxed himself. "Jesus, folks, some grasshoppers you can't save no matter what you do. Look, Berta, you don't have to go to school! You don't have to do anything! You don't even have to work, but you've got to be *some*where, so why not . . ."

"Chevy, I don't think so." She touched her finger to the protrudent red felt tongue of the bear.

"Why not?" He knew he should not press. He knew it. "Why not?" he said. "How come?"

"I don't think . . ."

"You don't *think* . . . C'mon, Berta, do better than that. Concrete reasons, please. One two three. Alphabetical order." He was marvelously gay, but all she could manage was to shake her head, and Chevy felt thick, heavy anger rise in him.

Then they both heard Beanie swing through the kitchen door and come down the aisle. He set a half-carton of milk and a glass in front of Chevy.

"On the housh," Beanie said. He squinted toward the door, as if talking to someone else down the row of stools.

"Gotta git rid of it or it'll shpoil," he explained to the empty seats.

"C'mon, Beanie, don't give me that," Chevy said. "You just have a big heart. We all know about it. A heart as big as all outdoors." Chevy poured and drank one full glass of milk without a pause, one hand pressing his stomach. "It's warm," he said. "Ah, Beanie, you know how to melt me. Warm, sour milk."

Beanie continued to stare down the aisle. He sat on one of the stools opposite the booth. Finally he swept his gaze across them. "Wha'd that cosht you?" he sneered toward the panda. ". . . 'bout ten bucksh?"

"Free, Beanie," Chevy said. "They're giving them away at the gate with free kisses for the gentlemen and flowers for the ladies. Alberta ate hers."

"Goddamn fairs," Beanie said. "Come to town and drain out all the money." He gestured toward the empty stools. "Don't bring no businesh. Just suck out all the money and leave. Don't put a whuckin' penny in and take it all out. Three daysh now." He smacked his lips and shook his head, a businessman in trouble.

"Be of stout heart, Beanie," Chevy said. "By morning there will be only empty Coke cups and cotton candy sticks to prove they were ever here. Again Beanie's Chili Parlor will resound with the happy melody of the cash register."

Alberta mounted her panda on the juke box selector and left him to ride there. She licked a palm and shook a little salt into it and then touched her tongue to the salt. Chevy and Beanie watched this closely.

"Hey, Beanie, guess what," she said, dipping her head

toward the salt again, chicken-like and not looking up. "Chevy's been offered a job teaching at the University of Michigan."

"Just an assistantship," Chevy explained. He poured more milk. "I'll be going to school too."

"Yeah?" Beanie said cautiously. He began to look closely at Alberta, not swinging on the stool any more. "Michigan," he scoffed. "Couldn't git me to live there. Cold! Windy! Tornadosh! Goddamn shmog! It ain't pretty in Michigan," he said. "Shiddy there."

"You been to Michigan, Beanie?" Alberta asked.

Beanie looked away, pained "Shee-it!" he said. Such questions were left unanswered.

"I heard it was neat," she said, dipping again toward the salt.

"You heard of De*troit?*" Beanie asked. To Beanie Detroit had the same flavor as the plague, gonorrhea, Alcatraz. "Detroitsh in Michigan," he informed her.

Chevy rolled the empty milk glass between his hands. Alberta dipped again toward the salt. In the kitchen one of the freezers switched on. Beanie began to swing back and forth again on the stool. He reached a finger and thumb behind one ear, pinched briefly and brought the hand back around to see, curious at what he had found. He brushed finger and thumb against his apron. "You don't wanna go to Goddamn whuckin' *Mich*igan," he said to Alberta.

"Beanie, I said *Chevy's* going to Michigan."

Beanie looked at Chevy. "Shee-it," he said again, and he left his stool and returned to the kitchen.

Alberta licked the remaining salt, then looked up, meeting and holding Chevy's eyes for a moment before she spoke. "It's been a good day," she said. "It really has, hasn't it. A good summer too."

"Yeah, it has." Chevy began to roll his milk glass again.

"I'm gonna miss you, Chevy. I wish there were a way to do this so you didn't miss people. I'm gonna miss you a lot."

"I know a way," he said, still looking at the glass. "Come with me. Come on, Berta. Why not?"

"Chevy," she said in an unnatural voice. "Don't. Help me out. I don't know how to do these things. I'm no good at it."

They heard Beanie come again through the kitchen door. He came quickly, as if he had things to say or do, important things, but when he sat again on his stool he was silent. He began to swing nervously back and forth in quarter-circles. Alberta took her panda down from its mount on the selector and stood it in front of her on the table — the two, bear and girl, staring blankly at one another, one with stitched mouth eternally smiling.

"Somesing's gonna happen," Beanie blurted. "I feel bad." He looked down the aisle, shivering suddenly and grabbing his own shoulders with his hands as if a cold wind had just blown over him. "Bad news ish comin'."

Chevy and Alberta were silent.

"I sink Harrish is comin' back," Beanie said.

"Who?" Chevy said.

"Harrish."

"Beanie," Alberta said, not unkindly, "If Harris was alive he'd have been back here years ago."

"*Some*sing!" Beanie said. He swung around on his stool

to face the counter, his back turned to them, then after a second he spun back. "I sink I'll buy a whuckin' TeeVee for in here," he said. He brushed his eyes past Alberta to see what effect this might have on her, but she had not reacted at all. She continued to stare at the panda.

"One of them big color whuckers," he said.

Still no reaction.

" 'Bout five hunner for one of them big color whuckers," he said. "Put it on a platform about right there." He pointed with his whole arm. It was impossible not to see the direction.

"About half the people ain't gonna be able to see it up there, Beanie," Alberta said.

"I ain't buyin' it for no whuckin' cushtomer," he said.

"Who you buying it for, Beanie?"

"*Me*, by God!"

"Then why don't you put it out in the kitchen?"

Beanie began to spin again on the stool for a moment. "Shmart-ash bitsh," he said, and he left again for the kitchen.

Chevy saw Alberta bring the panda close to her face as if to kiss it, and when she held it there for several moments he realized that she was hiding tears.

"He'll do okay, Berta," he said.

She took a breath. "I know."

"He'll be cussing you in a week."

"I know," she said.

"But what about me, Berta? What about me?"

Alberta shook her head, her face still pressed to the panda.

"Come with me, Berta. Come on! Why not?"

Alberta spoke slowly. "I'm not gonna say you're wrong going to Michigan, Chevy. I think it's fine for you. I really do. But don't say I'm wrong not going."

Chevy started to say something, but he did not.

"There's another way, you know," she said. "Come with *me*."

Again Chevy almost spoke, but he did not.

Then Alberta's face appeared from behind the panda. It looked up and slightly to the right, smiling a damp, tentative smile. "I just wanted to put the choice back in his hands, folks," she said. "I just wanted him to know that he could if he wanted to."

Chevy shook his head slowly. "You never forget a thing, do you?"

"Had a good teacher," she said. "And I believed everything he told me."

For a long time Chevy just looked at her, an expression on his face that was not quite a smile, but there was no line between his eyebrows. "Well, Alberta," he said finally. "I'm gonna go now." He looked at her, hesitating, then rose and left the booth.

At the door she called to him.

"Hey, Chevy," she said, and she was smiling, holding the bear to her chest. "Hey, don't marry any virgins, okay?"

Chevy spread his arms toward the ceiling and he lifted his eyes. "Folks . . ." he said. "Folks . . ." But he could think of nothing to tell them.